This Tomser Cat Book Belongs To:

_____

_____

See if you can spot Tomser Cat
hiding somewhere in the pages of this book!

To Lizzie with much Love

First published in 2017 by Tomser Cat Books
Ty Mawr House
Bryn Henwysg
Troedrhiw-Trwyn
Pontypridd CF37 2SE

www.tomsercat.com

Text copyright © Mark Dorey 2017
Illustrations copyright © Liz Dorey 2017
Moral rights asserted

A CIP catalogue record for this book is available
from the British Library

ISBN: 978-0-9927621-7-9

Printed in Great Britain

Polly's Magic Bubbles

Revenge of the Spiders

Mark Dorey

illustrated by Liz Dorey

Tomser Cat Books

Other brilliant books by Mark & Liz Dorey

Cougars (for adventurers 7 to 11)

Polly's Magic Bubbles and the Quest for Dizzelwood

*The Mystery of the Un-Snowy Mountain
and the
Great Deep Sleep Miscalculation*

Big Cats (young adults and older adventurers too)

*The Extraordinary Happenings of Peter Oddfellow:
The Old Umbrella*

Mousers (picture books for our youngest readers)

Can We Walk to the Moon?

How High Do Trees Grow?

The Story of How God Un-Invisibled Himself

Help! I'm Lost Property!

Also available from Tomser Cat Books

The Green Eyes of Darkness by Michael C Thomas

Ballerina by Emily Hancox

Many thanks to
Ysgol Evan James, Pontypridd
for helping to choose the final *Polly* cover!
and last but certainly not least
Richie, Katie, Gary, Colin & Ted for all your help and feedback!

Polly's Magic Bubbles
Revenge of the Spiders

Chapter One

Being Followed...

Polly thought she was being followed.

Polly sensed she was being followed.

Polly **knew** she was being followed.

There were other kids walking home from school on the opposite side of the road and they were definitely not following her.

But someone, or worse still, *something* was.

Polly tried her absolute best not to glance over her shoulder, but the skitterings in her stomach were getting worse and worse – *she just had to know*. She tried half-looking, almost, sort of, but not quite just innocently turning her head, but even that was no good. She couldn't see anything.

The longer she walked, the more certain she became. Something was there, and it was following her.

What she needed was a good look. A very definite 'turn around and look' look. But deep down, Polly was too afraid of what she might discover if she did look.

If only Marcia were here. Of all the times for her best friend to be ill.

SHE NEEDED MARCIA NOW!

Polly was on her own with someone or *something* following her. She slipped her right hand into her pocket, scrabbling with desperate fingers.

Empty.

Trying not to panic, she plunged her left hand into her other pocket.

Empty.

Wait a minute – *what was she searching for?*

Unable to answer her own question, Polly weighed up her options, quickly realising that short of breaking into a run (and who knew what might happen then?), there was really only one other option left. She would have to turn around and confront whatever it was.

Polly slowed, taking a deep breath as she quietly built up her resolve. Before she could change her mind, she decided that she would spin around on a count of three...

One... Two... Three!

Polly spun on her heel.

No one was there. Well, not quite no one.

A squirrel – looking more like a skunk than a squirrel – stood motionless about twenty feet away, looking every bit as startled as Polly was. In the endless seconds that followed, the nine-year-old and the skunk-squirrel stared at each other. Then in a flash it was gone, scampering up a nearby tree at the side of the road.

The skitterings in her stomach now gone, Polly turned to continue on her way home with a new lightness in her step.

Then, without warning, the skitterings returned.

There was something else about the squirrel.

But what was it?

Polly turned again.

The skunk-squirrel was nowhere to be seen.

DANGER! DANGER! DANGER!

An overwhelming and unrelenting sense of menace gripped her, its cold fingers squeezing tighter and tighter...

Some boys across the road were shouting and messing about, up to their typical boy nonsense. Slowly, deliberately, Polly began to approach the tree, all the time scanning its leafy canopy; the leaves quite, quite still.

Wait... a movement, just up and to the left.

Polly pushed her shivering senses aside as she took a few more steps. Standing right next to the tree trunk, she became transfixed by the sunlight dancing and mottling its knobbly bark.

Something caught her peripheral vision.

There it was again.

A definite movement.

Red, glowing eyes peered, sharp and defiant from the clumps of leafy green.

Then down it came. A mass of legs and a giant black bulbous body. The spider was already weaving a large web, impossibly quickly. The silken net entrapped her.

Unable to move, Polly looked on helplessly as the spider closed in, dark eyes blazing with hatred as its giant pincers clicked with deadly menace.

Polly tried to scream.

TOO LATE!

Another web gagged her mouth.

Gasping for breath, Polly fell to the floor wondering what on earth was going to happen next...

Chapter Two

A MESSING WITH TIME

Polly stared at the ceiling.

She was in her bed with no sign of spiders or creepy squirrels anywhere to be seen.

What a strange dream!

Polly looked towards the window, still a little breathless, her heartbeat racing. She closed her eyes to try and calm herself.

DISASTER!

Giant spiders imprinted like dark shadows crawled along the insides of her eyelids. Opening her eyes, Polly just lay there as motionless as possible, letting her heart begin to slow back to its normal rhythm.

The nightmare firmly behind her, Polly sat up, brushing her hair away from her face. Something snagged her mouth. Polly's eyes grew wide in horror as she pulled at the slender thread.

It wasn't a dream after all – it was real!

Polly tried not to panic.

She needed help. She would go and see Marcia. Then she remembered, her best friend was still unwell. Polly strengthened her resolve – she would go and see her anyway. This was an emergency.

There was a knock on the door.

"Pol?" Jake's voice sounded from behind the door. Her older brother rarely talked to her, and even less so since becoming a teenager. "Pol, it's Dad!"

Polly hurried to the door, swinging it open. Jake's greasy face bobbed up and down nervously on his scrawny neck, beneath a mop of unkempt hair.

"What's up with Dad?"

Jake stared.

"Jake, what's up with Dad?"

Her brother was pointing, staring intently, almost mesmerised. "You've got something hanging from your mouth. Is that a spi—?"

"For goodness sake, Jake, it doesn't matter what it is! What's up with Dad?"

"Oh, nothing really, he's lost his pipe and was wondering if you'd seen it."

Polly stared at her brother, incredulously. *"Is that it?"*

"Yeah, guess so," shrugged Jake, a little sheepishly.

Polly slammed the door.

Dad's pipe was his most treasured possession and a bit of a curiosity, even by pipe standards. Obviously very old, it was quite long and intricately carved with what looked like vines winding all along the pipe stem, eventually wrapping themselves around an over-sized bowl. On each side of the pipe bowl, small faces could be seen peeping out from behind the vines, happy on the one side and angry on the other. The inside of the pipe bowl was unusual in that not only was it spotless with no evidence of ever having been 'smoked', but also it had funny swirly patterns carved on the inside, like some sort of ancient writing.

Dad had been drawn to the pipe as soon as he spotted it in an old antique shop when Mum, Dad and a very young Jake were on holiday, and Mum was pregnant with Polly. Dad loved walking around with the pipe in his mouth, puffing away even though he never put tobacco in it. Mum insisted that Dad's 'pipe romance', as she called it, had something to do with his liking for dressing in antiquated tweed waistcoats and jackets (always bought from charity shops), and watching old black and white movies whenever he got the chance.

Both Polly and her Mum suspected that Dad had a secret yearning to be a 1920s college professor, and his pipe and old-fashioned clothes were the closest he ever came to achieving his ambition. Despite all his quirkiness, everyone was secretly relieved that Dad kept his pipe unlit – there would be nothing worse than Dad going around puffing like an old steam engine filling the house with pongy pipe fumes.

Polly extracted the sticky spider strand from her mouth for a closer look.

Was the dream just a coincidence?

'You can never be too sure of spiders!' whispered a strange voice.

Polly spun around.

No one was there.

Was she dreaming again?

Could this be a dream inside a dream?

Was anything ever going to make sense?

Polly pinched herself. **OUCH!**

Definitely not a dream! The spider's web was real, her brother was real, and as for Dad's missing pipe, well, who really cared where that was.

'The spiders are real too!'

The whispering voice from nowhere was starting to freak her out.

There was another knock on the door.

Polly nearly yanked the door off its hinges. "What is it now, Jak—!?"

"Spiders are real too," said the man, doffing his battered top hat. "Have you seen—?"

Polly slammed the door shut, throwing her full weight against it just to make sure.

Who on earth was the strange old man on the other side of the door in the ill-fitting suit?

Where was Marcia when she needed her? Not that Marcia would know what to do. If anything, Marcia would most probably do something really stupid like inviting the old man in for some tea and biscuits!

Polly's head was spinning with lots of questions that desperately needed some answers. Gathering herself, she turned the door knob as slowly and as quietly as she possibly could. Then slowly... ever so slowly... she began opening the door, millimetre by careful millimetre...

Peering through the small opening and ready to slam the door at the slightest hint of danger, Polly scanned through the sliver of a gap with desperate eyes.

The old man was gone.

In his place was Mum – a very annoyed Mum.

"What on earth is all this slamming of doors?"

"Sorry, I thought you were someone else."

Mum remained unimpressed. "And who else would that be exactly?"

"An old man."

"The only 'old man' around here is your father," Mum rubbed her fingers along the doorframe. "I don't believe it, even more cobwebs!"

Polly's heart skipped a beat.

"While you've been busy having your peculiar imaginings, we've had spiders spinning their nasty webs here, there and everywhere!"

"He was rather strange..." mused Polly. "Strange but familiar..."

"You need to stop daydreaming, my girl, and do something useful, like helping us find a certain 'old man's' pesky pipe for a start!"

Polly scarcely heard what her Mum was saying, lost as she was in her own thoughts.

Spiders were everywhere.

She hadn't been dreaming at all.

It was real.

Polly's Mum turned to leave. "I'd better get back downstairs before Joshy starts tearing the place apart with those mischievous fingers of his, especially with all these nasty, dirty cobwebs everywhere!"

Joshy, Polly's younger brother, was an incredibly active three-year-old who liked nothing better than getting his little fingers into just about anything and everything whenever and wherever he had the chance.

Polly wasn't sure what to do. Dad's pipe definitely wasn't a priority, but she knew that she should do something... *but what?*

13

'Time is of the essence!'

Polly reeled around.

Nothing.

'Time is of the essence?'

What was that supposed to mean?

Then, as if to amplify the question bouncing around in all the chaos of her head, Polly's bedroom clock began to tick LOUDER and s-l-o-w-e-r.

Polly glanced at the clock. It was nearly 9am, but the second hand had almost stopped moving.

'Time is of the essence!'

WHAT WAS HAPPENING?

'Time is of the essence...'

'... and timing is everything!'

Everything stopped.

The clock. The world. Everything.

Polly didn't know how or why, it just did.

A blanket of quiet covered everything – a quietness she'd never experienced before.

A time-standing-still quietness.

She rushed to her bedroom window.

Nothing moved.

Everything was still.

The trees were still.

Polly opened her bedroom window.

The wind was still.

She listened.

Nothing. Nothing at all.

Everything was quite, quite still.

'Timing is everything!'

Polly could hear her heart thumping in her chest — at least *she* was still working!

She closed the window, deep in thought. Cobwebs... missing pipes... strange voices... even stranger people... and now the stopping of time itself.

What was happening???

Was she the only one experiencing this or were there others trapped in this time-less phenomenon?

Polly reopened her window.

Nothing.

No traffic. No birdsong. No wind. No nothing.

BUBBLES.

Why this sudden thought flashed into her mind was like everything else that was happening around her, a complete mystery.

BUBBLES.

Why was she suddenly thinking of bubbles?

Something moved — not outside, but inside.

Inside Polly's head.

A dark veil of forgetfulness lifted slightly as Polly started to remember.

A hazy recollection of some bubbles she had maybe bought – *were they bought or were they given to her?* Pieces of stray thoughts started to float around her head, slowly coming together: *The bubbles were in a tiny container, but where did she get them from?* Not that it mattered anyway, Polly couldn't remember where she'd put them, or even if they'd ever existed in the first place. She began to pull open all her cupboard doors and drawers, but the half-remembered bubbles were nowhere to be seen.

Where was that silly little bottle?

Polly trawled through some boxes under her bed.

Nothing. Maybe she'd imagined the whole thing.

But why on earth would she possibly imagine something as random as a tiny bottle of bubbles?

Why was everything so weird?

Polly scanned her bedroom for spiders or telltale webs or anything else that might help her.

Nothing.

It was then that she saw it.

A glow.

16

A strange golden light was coming from one of Polly's shoes just beneath her bookshelf. Carefully picking it up and holding it at arm's length, Polly shook the shoe, cautiously.

A tiny green bottle with a gold top that shone like the sun rattled down into the heel.

The whole curiosity was wrapped in old yellowing paper. Carefully extracting the bottle, Polly unwrapped the weathered paper. The words scrawled on it screamed off the parchment:

Time is of the Essence...

Polly stared at the words in disbelief.

Then she heard a sound. The slow ticking of a clock. The second hand was moving again.

Time is of the essence...

She looked back at the paper. The paper was blank.

She turned it over and over in her hands.

Blank.

No, something was happening, something weird and frighteningly wonderful.

Different words started to appear:

...and timing is Everything!

The clock ticking volume increased, getting

Louder and LOUDER...

then *faster...*

and *faster...*

and *faster...*

Polly stared open-mouthed as the second hand of the clock whizzed around impossibly fast, dragging the minute hand along in its wake.

Then, without rhyme or reason, time swiftly decided to go back to normal.

9:46am.

Suddenly, there was a knock on the door.

Chapter Three

COBWEBS!

"**S**piders!" Jake stood in the doorway, his face ashen.

A chill surged down Polly's back like an icy express train. With the tiny bubble container clenched tightly in her hand, she charged past her brother. Stopping suddenly, Polly looked on in horror at the sight before her. Cobwebs were strung and strewn everywhere, getting increasingly more dense as she peered down the stairs.

"I just came out of my room..." said Jake, bewildered and stunned. "Something weird's happening here, Pol."

Polly scanned the cobwebby chaos – at least there were no spiders. She started to make her way downstairs.

"Pol, where are you going?"

Polly turned, fixing her older brother with her best annoyed stare. "Where does it look like I'm going?"

Before Jake could reply, Polly began shoving her way steadily through the masses of sickly sticky strands.

Downstairs was deathly silent. Taking a deep breath, Polly pushed the living room door which was now matted in a thick net of cobwebs. The door was stuck. Polly tried again, but the door was jammed solid.

"Do you think you could stop gawping and start helping?" Polly's words stung Jake into action, and together they managed to inch the door open, sticky spider strands stretching and snapping before streaming down the sides of the door like grotty grey gruesome candy floss.

Steeling herself, Polly peered around the door into the living room. Everywhere and everything was smothered in crusty cobwebs: furniture, light fittings, the TV and even Granny's old piano. But worst and most terrible by far, Mum and Dad and little Joshy were all cocooned with layers and layers of creepy-crawly spider webs and looking like waxwork statues.

"I was only gone a minute," said Jake, trailing after his sister into the barely recognisable room. "I was looking for Dad's pipe in my room. Do you think they're—"

Ignoring her brother, Polly pressed her way through the cobweb chaos, each sticky strand clinging to her jeans as she ploughed her way towards the three figures now in suspended animation.

Brushing aside the filthy webs, Polly reached out. Mum, Dad and Joshy were still warm, and although completely motionless, they were breathing. Polly heaved a sigh of relief. A quick scan of the web-filled room revealed no sign of any spiders.

Would the spiders be coming back, and if so, what were they after?

She clenched her hand around the tiny container as Jake hovered behind her like a useless shadow. "Jake, did you see anything, anything at all?"

"I was looking in my bedroom."

Polly thought of asking why would their Dad's pipe be in Jake's bedroom, but there were more important questions. "What about anything else, you know, like *spiders*, or *squirrels* maybe?"

Jake shook his head in dumbstruck slow motion.

Polly could feel the growing fountain of panic rising from the pit of her stomach and threatening to erupt in a scream if she opened her mouth to let it. Unclenching her hand, she stared at the minuscule bubble container. Somehow, this was all about the bubbles. How she knew this she wasn't sure, but she knew it better than she knew anything – those meddlesome spiders and the bubbles were somehow connected.

"What's that in your hand?"

Polly ignored her brother's question. "We need to get help."

"Yeah sure, and how do you think we're going to explain all this to the police?"

"We're not going to explain anything, and we're not calling the police."

"But—"

"We need Marcia."

"But—?"

"Jake, are you with me or not?"

Jake had never seen his little sister so determined – maybe a bit bossy sometimes, especially when he had his nose in one of his magazines or books and she wanted him to do something, but this was a different Polly, a side of her that he'd never seen before. But then again, everything that was happening was weird, and even as an avid reader, Jake had never read about anything like this before in his life.

Jake weighed up the options and quickly realised that there weren't any.

"Guess so," he muttered, not really knowing what else to say and definitely not keen on staying in the house on his own.

Marcia's Mum was rather shocked to see Polly and her brother standing at her front door. She began to inform them her daughter was not feeling very well, but on seeing the look on Polly's face, she changed her mind and allowed them to go upstairs – but only for a quick visit. She started to say something else, but Polly and Jake were already up the stairs, heading straight for Marcia's bedroom.

Marcia was sitting up in bed, looking quite glum but she brightened immediately when she saw Polly. Her expression changed to one of shock as Jake trailed in after her.

"It's a long story," said Polly, plonking herself down on the end of Marcia's bed. "How are you feeling?"

Marcia reached across to grab a 'magic slate' from her bedside table and began to write:

I've lost my voice!

"That's a relief," muttered Jake under his breath.

Polly shot her brother a scornful look as Marcia swiped the slate's magnet across its surface to scribble something else.

"Marcia, listen, this is important."

Marcia stopped mid-scribble.

"Our house has been overrun with spiders, lots of them, and I think they are something to do with these." Polly thrust out her hand holding the tiny container. "The thing is, I can't figure out what the connection is."

Marcia's eyes grew wide, her blonde curls quivering with excitement as she hastily scrawled on her magic slate.

I remember!

"You do?"

Sort of – but not quite!

"What's that supposed to mean?"

I think you should blow one.

"What's going on?" asked Jake, "I thought we were supposed to be helping Mum, Dad and Joshy."

"We are, or at least we're trying to." Polly began unscrewing the shimmering gold top.

"Oh yeah, of course – blowing some teeny-tiny bubbles is going to help loads!"

Polly glared at her brother. "It's better than doing nothing."

"Wow, I wish I'd thought of that. Our family's trapped under masses of creepy cobwebs and all we have to do is blow some stupid little bubb—"

Polly began to blow, Jake staring gobsmacked as the tiny bubble grew Bigger...

and Bigger...

and BIGGER...

"WHOA!" Both Jake and Polly gawped at the huge bubble in disbelief, their astonishment broken by Marcia, who was grunting and pointing frantically.

Something was happening to the bubble. A face was beginning to form on its soapy surface. A crookedy nose broke through as a giant mouth yawned open, filling the air with skin-crawling crackly-cackling laughter.

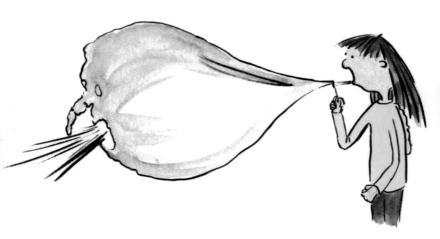

The giant freaky-face-bubble cackled as it bobbed around Marcia's bedroom.

"HA!" "HA!" "HA!"
"HA!" "HA!"
"HA!" "HA!" "HA!"
"HA!" "HA!" "HA!"

With each passing second, the hideous bubble grew

Bigger...

and BIGGER...

and BIGGER...

The horrid bubble face expanded larger and larger, its sinister laugher growing

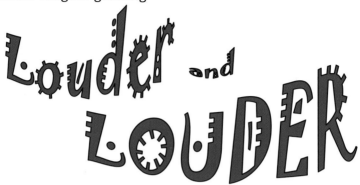

Louder and LOUDER

as cobwebby strands began to form all over its surface.

BANG

The bubble exploded, depositing soapy cobweb strands everywhere.

"*YUCK!* Did that just happen?" Jake was doing his best not to show that he was shaking.

"Yes," said Polly, a trembling mass herself, "unfortunately it did!"

"Lucky it burst."

"Luck had nothing to do with it!" Polly held up the tiny bubble blower which resembled a crooked sewing needle. "I used this."

Marcia was scribbling.

Sor-Ben-Rez → Dribblewood

Everything suddenly flooded back in a mental tidal wave, nearly knocking poor Polly off her feet. Sor-Ben-Rez was the evil stick man and Spider Lord who tried to capture the Magic Bubbles in order to take over Dizzelwood, the secret magical woodland. The nasty ex-Head Counsel and Advisor to the King and Queen of Dizzelwood had only been thwarted at the very last moment by Polly and Marcia's quick thinking, trapping him forever (or so they had thought), in a double-bubble-skinned fireball. Both girls had presumed Sor-Ben-Rez was eternally banished and no longer a threat, but the return of the spiders and now the bubble apparition suggested otherwise. If Sor-Ben-Rez and his spiders were on the loose, that meant only one thing:

TROUBLE...

BIG TROUBLE!

What was it that was written on the paper?
Something about time...
Polly unravelled the crumpled piece of paper:

Please take great care of your
Magic Bubbles!
FOR EMERGENCY USE ONLY!!!
Hopefully see you again soon!

The writing began to fade until the paper was blank.
"We have to go back."
"Back?" Jake was started nervously pacing around the room. "Back where?"
Marcia tapped on her slate. Dribblewood
"Dribblewood? Where's Dribblewood?"
"It's Dizzelwood, Jake, and don't worry, you can stay here – me and Marcia will go."
I can't go anywhere!

"I thought you said you were feeling better?"

I am, but I can't speak!

"Marcia, I don't need you to speak, *I just need you!* Now, are you with me or not?"

Marcia thought for a moment, then a big grin broke out across her face. **I'll need to get changed.**

"Jake, turn around."

Her brother started to protest.

"Now!"

Jake reluctantly spun to face the door as Marcia pulled on a pink top with blue leggings.

Polly groaned. "Don't you have anything more suitable?"

I have to look my best.

"Okay," sighed Polly. "Let's go."

"*Go?* We're not going anywhere!" exclaimed Jake. "Pol, unless you've forgotten, she's supposed to be ill and besides, we'll never get her out the door without being seen."

"We're not going out the door," said Polly.

Jake saw the look in his sister's eyes. "Oh no," he groaned, shaking his head. "No, no, no! There's absolutely no way I'm climbing out of the window."

"You don't have to climb anywhere, you're staying here. This is a job for me and Marcia."

"I can't stay *here – it's a girl's room!* What if her mum comes up, what am I going to say?"

"I'm sure you'll think of something," Polly was already blowing another bubble.

"What are you doing now?"

"Transport."

"Transport??? Are you crazy?" Jake turned to Marcia for support, but she just nodded her head excitedly. "Pol, what about Mum, Dad and Joshy? We have to do something!"

"We are doing something, Jake. Now, you stay put until we're gone and then you can sneak out of the front door."

With her magic slate in hand, Marcia was already climbing inside the giant bubble, the thin translucent surface easily supporting her weight.

Jake stared wide-eyed. "But—"

"Jake, you have to trust me in this, it's the only way."

Jake thought for a moment. "I'm coming with you."

"WHAT?"

"The only way I'm sneaking anywhere is out with you." Jake could see his sister wasn't convinced. "Aw come on, Pol, Mum and Dad would kill me if I let you go floating off to Drogglewood on your own. We need to stick together, so that I can keep my eye on you."

Polly could see it was no use arguing. "Okay, climb in, but be careful, we've never tried it with three before."

Jake clambered into the bubble, his face a mixture of worry and amazement. Securing the gold top on the tiny green container, Polly joined her companions inside the bubble as it floated towards the wall.

Jake was looking exceedingly worried – their journey could be over before it had started!

Marcia scribbled a hasty note and gave Jake a smug look.

Don't worry, we're going through the wall!

"Through the wa—"

The bubble hit the wall and bounced back, but at least it didn't pop. Marcia stopped smiling.

"It's Sor-Ben-Rez," said Polly. Marcia looked confused. "He's somehow stopping us from going through the wall. Everyone start running to the left!" If Marcia was confused before, her brain was totally scrambled now. "We need to steer the bubble towards the window." Both Jake and Marcia were staring as if she was from outer space. "Stop gawping and start running!"

They all started running, with Marcia running the opposite way!

"My left, Marcia, not yours!"

Marcia quickly changed direction and in a matter of seconds, the bubble started moving towards the open window.

Their relief was short lived as the bubble became snagged in the window frame.

The bubble's too big!

"Wait here!" ordered Polly.

Carefully reaching through the bubble, Polly climbed back out into the bedroom, hoping that she wouldn't pop the fragile surface in the process. Easing the bottom of the bubble through proved easy enough, but not so the top, which was just out of Polly's reach. Dragging a chair across, Polly climbed up and reached over to press on top of the bubble. Suddenly, the chair slipped, causing Polly to crash through the bubble's surface, straight on top of her brother! Amazingly, the bubble remained intact.

"Careful!" bleated Jake.

Marcia, in the meantime, was looking extremely worried.

Spiders – Lots of them!

Following her best friend's gaze, Polly stared in horror and disbelief. Thousands of spiders were climbing up the drainpipes and all over the walls of the house. Polly exited the bubble with renewed urgency. Repositioning herself on the chair, she carefully eased the top of the bubble through the open window. All that was left now was the sides.

A loud scratching was coming from just outside Marcia's bedroom door. Fearing the worst, Polly darted across the room and creaked open the door. The hallway was a mass of spiders, crawling up the stairs and banister, covering everything in their spidery wake in a blanket of webs.

'Time is of the essence!'

Slamming the door shut, Polly rushed back across the room and set to work on the sides of the bubble – a few gentle presses should be enough. The scratching behind the door intensified.

Time was running out – Correction, time had run out.

Large spiders were squashing and squeezing themselves under the door, legs first followed by their dense black bodies squishing and squirming through the narrow gap. Four of the sinister creepy-crawlies were almost through.

HURRY!!!

Polly was out of options. "Quick, both of you, move towards the edges of the bubble!"

Jake stared his best *'Are you crazy?'* stare.

"JUST DO IT!"

Marcia and Jake sprang into action as slowly the wedged bubble inched itself out.

"Further, you need to go further!"

Already on the far side of the bubble, there was not a lot of room left for Marcia and Jake to manoeuvre.

"There's spiders everywhere in here!" urged Polly.

Both Jake and Marcia pressed against the outside of the giant bubble, each praying silently that it wouldn't suddenly give way and send them both to their doom.

The bubble was almost through; just a few more millimetres... Polly worked frantically, pressing and easing the translucent surface through the window.

Something moved on Polly's leg – *a large spider was crawling up her jeans.* Worse still, her foot was now secured to the floor in a mass of webbing.

Polly pulled and pulled. The webbing held firm.

Polly pulled with all her might, but she was stuck – well and truly stuck! Sensing something was wrong, Jake made his way back to her side of the bubble and reached through the bubble's surface.

"Pol, take my hand!"

Spiders began to swarm all over the outside of the bubble that was hanging out of the window.

Marcia was scribbling something.

"Marcia, put that stupid thing down and grab hold of my waist!" screamed Jake.

Marcia regarded him with rising panic.

"Now!"

Marcia wrapped her arms around Jake's waist.

The spider was crawling up Polly's top, its mouth foaming with menace.

"JAKE, HURRY!"

Jake leaned out of the bubble, hands outstretched. "Take my hands, Pol, and after three, pull...

"One...Two... Three!"

Polly, Jake and Marcia pulled with all their might, the webbing now beginning to

STRETCH

and

STRETCH

and

STRE

Polly was catapulted into the bubble sending all three companions tumbling.

Fortunately, the bubble held.

Unfortunately, the spider was now in the bubble too! Almost up to Polly's neck, its mandibles

clackity
clack
clacking

with extreme menace.

Polly opened her mouth to scream...

Using her slate, Marcia swatted the spider through the surface of the bubble back into the bedroom, out of harm's way.

The top of the bubble was now encrusted with spider webs as it broke away from the window and floated free. With multitudes of spiders swarming and teeming menacingly across its sheer transparent surface, the three companions inside held their breath. The only thing now keeping them safe was just a few microns of soapy liquid.

Chapter Four

BUBBLE TROUBLE!

"What are we going to do about them?" Jake stared in horror at the hordes of scurrying spiders gnawing and web weaving their way around the outside of their bubble sanctuary.

Can they get through? scribbled Marcia.

"I'm sure we'll be okay," replied Polly, not really sure of how okay that might be, and completely unsure of how much spider abuse the bubble could take.

"So, where are we going, sis?"

"The bubble knows," answered Polly.

"I guess that's code for you don't know then."

"Yes... er... no! All I know is the bubble will take us where we need to go." Polly really had no idea what was happening, but felt she had to trust in something.

The bubble was rapidly becoming swathed in cobwebs, although they could still see out. Far below, Polly's house and half her street were now submerged in cobwebs as the cruel tide of black spiders crawled and swarmed everywhere!

What if she was wrong?

What if they were floating aimlessly skywards whilst thousands and thousands and thousands of creepy spiders were rampaging everywhere?

But the biggest question of all remained unanswered: *What were the spiders doing and what did they want?*

The answer materialised suddenly, filling her whole being: **The Magic.**

She slipped her hand into her pocket, wrapping her fingers around the small container.

MY HOUSE! Marcia's worried look echoed the sickness that Polly felt deep inside.

Polly rested a hand on her friend's arm. "Everything will be all right," she promised with a certainty she didn't feel. "All we have to do is stick together."

The Crystal floated in the air, its eerie light shimmering in the gloom, casting sinister shadows on unseen walls.

Sor-Ben-Rez peered into the Crystal's depths, his eager eyes seeing all the events unfolding clearly as they happened.

His spider army was doing well.

It had been a long, agonising and miserable journey of unending days, with every minute of every day like an eternity, ensnared in a seemingly inescapable prison combination of Magic Bubble and Fireball. Sor-Ben-Rez had seethed as the Kingdom – *his Kingdom* – had been cruelly wrenched from his grasp and restored to that nincompoop King and his Queen. It had taken nearly all his knowledge, strength and magical prowess – not to mention a considerable amount of fortune and luck, but the former Head Counsel and Royal Advisor had finally managed to escape and regroup, re-amassing his faithful spider troops to his unfinished cause. He clenched his fists, unaware that his nails were raking deep splinters in his bark-like skin.

Now it was only a matter of time. Soon he would be back to his full power. Sor-Ben-Rez refocused his thoughts and attention on the Crystal, his magic portal and all-seeing eye into the world.

He allowed himself a self-satisfied smile. Already the Magic was on its way and it would soon be back in his grasp. Then revenge would be his. He would extinguish those two meddlesome girls and the older boy. He licked his lips with relish. How they would die he hadn't yet decided – quickly or slowly, it didn't matter – the final outcome would be the same, the rest was just detail. Deliciously dark detail, but mere detail.

The Magic would soon be his.

Fully and rightfully his.

His to control.

His to subvert.

His.

The Mechanism was on its way and would soon be here. With both the Mechanism and the Magic firmly in his grasp, he would be invincible. All powerful. The King and Queen could keep their petty Woodland — at least for a while — Sor-Ben-Rez would ensure it was the last place to fall. He relished the prospect of the King and Queen looking on helpless, as not only their precious land, but the whole world crumbled around them under his unyielding might.

He was getting ahead of himself. One thing at a time. First the Mechanism, then the Magic. Sor-Ben-Rez turned his gleeful attention to the three unsuspecting companions drifting ever closer.

Not long now. Everything was coming together.

The former Head Counsel waved his hand. The image in the Crystal darkened and shifted. His spider army had done well, almost too well, but at least the three had escaped. He would have preferred just the two, but the boy was of no great concern — their end would be the same.

Sor-Ben-Rez grinned in the gloom as the Crystal image shifted back once more to the floating bubble.

Not long now...

Polly opened her eyes.

Both Marcia and Jake were staring at her.

"Are you all right, Pol?"

"Yeah, sure," said Polly, feeling far from all right.

"You were like a statue," said Jake.

Marcia nodded her agreement, her head a mass of wobbling curls.

"While you were away with the fairies, the cobwebs have got worse!"

Jake was right; two thirds of the bubble's surface was now covered in a dense sticky mass of cobwebs.

"Soon we won't be able to see anything at all."

"We're being watched," said Polly, her words hanging in the air like a bad smell.

"Watched?"

What do you mean?

"Someone's watching us."

Jake stared at his sister, incredulously. "What, all the way up here, miles in the sky?"

Sor-Ben-Rez

Polly nodded. "I don't know how, but Mr Creepy is keeping his eye on us and... "

Jake and Marcia waited for her to finish.

"... and we're heading straight back to him."

"Wait a minute – are you saying that that laughing

face we saw in the bubble is somehow behind all this and he's got his beady eye on us?"

"It explains why they're covering the bubble with cobwebs and not breaking through."

"Oh come on, Pol, we're miles up in the sky! If you think—"

"He's taking us captive, Jake, don't you see? He's taking us captive and bringing us back to him."

But aren't the bubbles on our side?

Polly shrugged.

"Back to where?" asked Jake. "Drizzlewood?"

"I don't think so, unless he's suddenly regained power. No, I don't think that's it — the King said something earlier about time."

"*The King?* What King? When?"

"Before all this stuff kicked off. When you were looking for Dad's pipe."

"There was a King in our house?"

Polly nodded. "I didn't recognise him at the time."

"Of course! A King turns up at our house and you didn't recognise him. I suppose he wasn't wearing his crown."

"He doesn't have a crown, Jake, he wears a hat."

"I see, a King with a hat. So what did you do when you met the King with a hat?"

"I slammed the door in his face."

"What?"

"I slammed the door in his face before he could say anything."

"You're not making sense. You just said that he said something about time."

"He did... but he wasn't there when he said it."

"How can a King who wasn't there start talking to you about time? Was he talking through the door or something?"

"No, he was talking... he was talking in my head."

"WHAT?"

"I know it sounds strange..."

Marcia held up her board. I believe her.

Jake stared in disbelief. "My sister's gone mad and you're saying you believe her?"

"Jake, I know it doesn't really make sense, but me and Marcia have been through something like this before, and one thing I do know, we have to get out of here before we're completely trapped and unable to do anything."

"Oh yeah, get out of here, right. We're miles up in the air surrounded by thousands of creepy spiders just dying to eat us and we've got to get out of here!"

"Not 'eat us', Jake, *trap us.*"

"Fine, let's get out then," scoffed Jake, his hands defiantly on his hips.

"Jake, be serious."

"I am serious, Pol, I haven't got a clue what to do!"

The Power of Two

"Yes!" cried Polly. "That's it, Marcia, you're a genius!"

"That's what...?" Jake was more confused than ever.

"Stand back, both of you, we're getting out of here." Taking out the tiny bubble container, Polly began unscrewing the shiny gold top. Jake began to say something, but Polly held up her hand. "Jake, please..."

Polly began to blow, a tiny bubble formed getting

Bigger...

and BIGGER...

and BIGGER...

"Marcia, quick, blow inside my bubble."

Marcia joined her best friend and blew, a second bubble now appearing inside the first: *Bigger...*

and BIGGER...

and BIGGER...

Soon, the double-skinned bubble was almost taking up the entire space inside the cobwebby bubble.

"Get inside," ordered Polly.

"What about you?"

"Don't worry about me, you and Marcia, inside. *Now!*"

Jake and Marcia pressed through into the double-skinned bubble. Once they were safely inside, Polly pushed through to join them.

"Now what?" asked Jake.

"We're leaving," said Polly steely eyed, "through there." She pointed at the rapidly diminishing portion of the outer bubble's surface yet to be covered in cobwebs. "We need to position our bubble so that it's in line."

After a lot of shifting and jiggling, the double-bubble was in place.

"Now, push!"

They all pushed together, the double-skinned bubble beginning to stretch through the still as yet un-cobwebbed portion of the outer bubble.

"Keep going!" urged Polly.

Slowly but surely, the double bubble began to emerge from the web-free portion of the outer bubble. Alert to their escape, spiders began to descend onto the new bubble now nearly half way out of the outer bubble. More and more spiders descended rapidly onto their emerging bubble, already spinning their sinister webs to trap them once more.

Polly clenched her fist and punched through the double-bubble.

The giant spider bubble exploded, sending hundreds and hundreds of hapless spiders to their doom in a mass of webs and legs. Jake stared at his sister in stunned admiration but Polly was in no mood for celebrating. Pulling back her hand, she screwed the needle-like bubble blower back onto the container.

New webs were already forming on the surface of their double bubble.

Polly was on her feet.

"RUN!"

Marcia and Polly started running. Slowly, their bubble began to rotate.

"Jake, we need all three of us," gasped Polly.

The three ran, the double bubble spinning ever faster, dislodging the desperately clinging spiders one by one, with some still dangling by their webby threads. Many of them were already beginning to reel themselves in to re-establish themselves on the bubble's surface.

"I've got an idea," shouted Polly. "Keep running!"

Unscrewing the top of the small bottle, she rattled the blower inside the neck of the bottle to dispense any soapy liquid back into it. Cupping the blower in a clenched fist, Polly once again punched through the double skin, this time using the blower like a knife, cutting through the webby strands and sending the wretched spiders plummeting to their doom.

HOORAY!

Marcia's celebrations were cut short as Polly screamed! A spider was clamped onto Polly's out-stretched hand and viciously sinking his fangs into her. Determined not to lose her grip on the bubble blower, Polly re-clenched her fist as the spider's mandibles bit deeper and deeper.

"He's after the bubble blower, Pol, let it go!"

Polly glared at her brother. This was not an option even though she was in considerable pain. Taking hold of his sister's outstretched arm, Jake pulled with all his might. For some reason, everything except Polly's fist holding the blower was allowed back through the bubble's surface. Tears streamed down Polly's cheeks as the spider continued its merciless assault on her hand.

Grabbing Marcia's slate, Jake punched through the double surface, ready to swat the arachnid.

"No!" screamed Polly. "You'll make me drop the blower!"

Carefully re-angling the slate, Jake scraped along Polly's clenched fist, chiselling the spider loose with a desperate thrust. Polly pulled her hand back through, relieved to be free of the spider and more importantly still, to have possession of the bubble blower.

A croaky squeak came from behind.

Marcia was pointing.

Jake had retrieved the slate, but the spider had somehow cast a web at the last minute and was once again reeling itself in. Unable to penetrate the bubble's exterior, the spider glowered through the soapy surface with malevolent intent.

Unexpectedly, Polly thrust her injured clenched fist back through the double bubble surface. Seizing his chance for a second bite, the spider closed in, mandibles CLICK-CLACKING furiously.

Polly opened her fist, thrusting the blower deep into the spider's body. With mandibles clicking violently and all eight legs thrashing, Polly withdrew her hand, sending the dying spider tumbling to its doom.

From his hidden viewpoint, Sor-Ben-Rez smiled.

All was going to plan.

Chapter Five

STORM!

"**A**re you all right?" asked Jake.

Polly screwed the top back onto the small container and stowed the Magic Bubbles safely back in her pocket. All her energy now drained, Polly slumped, wincing as she shielded her injured hand.

Jake crouched down. "Maybe I should take care of the bubbles."

Polly met her brother's suggestion with a glare, the ferocity of which Jake had never seen before.

"Okay, have it your way – I was only trying to help." Are you OK?

Polly managed a half smile. "I'm okay, I guess. My hand's a bit sore, that's all."

"Let me take a look," offered Jake. Polly remained stock still. "Pol, you've got a bite. It might get infected."

Horrible thoughts of her hand swelling up and exploding in a gory mass of blood and tiny swarming spiders flooded Polly's imagination. She retched, her stomach churning as a sudden dizziness hit her like a wild storm cloud. Unable to protest any more, Polly reluctantly held out her injured hand.

"He's had a good old chomp, all right," Jake reached into his pocket took out a key fob. Deftly flicking out a small magnifying glass, he began to examine the two pock marks now glowing with an angry red.

"From what I can see... it looks like he only got you once."

Once is more than enough! thought Polly, but said nothing.

Marcia was scribbling.

How do you know it was a 'He'?

"I don't," replied Jake.

"Does it really matter what sex the spider was?" Polly had had more than enough of stupid spiders.

Marcia thought of writing something else, but then decided maybe not.

Jake was searching his pockets. "It's a shame we haven't got any bandages."

R~R~R~R~I~I~P~P~P!

Marcia tore a strip from her top. Then from some hidden pocket she produced a small plastic pink cupcake (with a cherry on the top).

"Marcia, what on earth...?"

Marcia held up a finger to silence Polly's question. Flicking up the top of the cupcake, Marcia dipped a finger and applied it to Polly's wound.

"Is that *lip balm*?" asked Polly, grimacing as the improvised ointment was rubbed in to the wound.

Marcia nodded. The balm stung, but only for a moment as Marcia expertly wrapped the wound with her makeshift pink bandage.

It felt good.

Polly smiled. "Thanks, Marcia," she said, meaning it.

"Looking good, sis!" grinned Jake. "You know, lip balm is brilliant for lots of things, not just bites and stings and small cuts." Both girls stared at him with their best *'What on earth could boys possibly know about lip balm?'* looks, but Jake was on a roll. "You can use lip balm to lubricate and loosen sticking zips and drawers and you can even waterproof or polish your shoes with it. It even can be used to fix scratches on CDs!" The girls continued to stare with a mixture of amazement and disbelief. "Seriously, lip balm's a great survival tool – I read somewhere that you can even make it into a candle using a matchstick as a wick," explained Jake, gazing out at the blue expanse. "I wish I'd brought a book or at least a pair of binoculars..."

The storm came out of nowhere, the wind rising from barely a whisper to a raging, howling gale in a matter of minutes. Rain swamped the bubble in a thunderous deluge before giving way to hailstones which battered the outside of the double bubble. Many of the freezing white balls penetrated the bubble's outer skin, but fortunately not the inner one.

Then came the thunder and lightning; its forking fingers of frighteningly bright light assaulting them from all sides, threatening to pierce their fragile floating transport.

Marcia cowered in Polly's arms. Not for the first time, Polly was relieved that her best friend had lost her voice, as she felt certain that Marcia would have let out an ear-piercing scream every time the thunder rumbled or the lightning flashed. Meanwhile, Jake just stared out from the confines of the bubble in complete silence. Polly wasn't sure whether her brother was scared or fascinated by all that was happening, but knowing Jake, she suspected it was a mixture of both. Had it not been for the trembling Marcia and the severe bubble buffeting, Polly might have been a little more fascinated herself, but then again, perhaps not – her mind, like the bubble, was being buffeting too, her head swimming full of unanswered questions:

Where were they heading?

What were the spiders up to?

Where was the King?

And perhaps the biggest, most important (and most terrifying) question of all:

Where was Sor-Ben-Rez and what was his dastardly part in all this?

Another rattling rumble of thunder shook the bubble as lightning forked much too close for comfort. Polly's questions would have to wait for another time. She was beginning to doubt the safety of the bubble, even if it was double-skinned. Glancing over at Jake, it was clear that he too was having similar thoughts.

Polly lifted the bandage to peek at her wound. The area around the spider bite was slightly swollen, but apart from that, she felt little if any discomfort at all. Marcia's lip balm was working!

Polly thought about the strangeness of it all.

Here she was, floating miles in the sky in a giant bubble. The last time she had been in this position, it was just her and Marcia, but that seemed like a lifetime ago. All those incredible adventures and yet somehow, she and Marcia had let them drift from their memories. How they could have possibly forgotten, Polly had no idea, but forgotten they had.

Now, here she was again, this time with her brother in tow; a brother she hardly ever spoke two words to (except maybe at Christmas or on birthdays)! It wasn't that Polly didn't want to speak to Jake, it's just that he always had his nose firmly embedded in one of his books or magazines. The simple fact was, Jake never talked or spoke to anyone unless he really had to. Polly smiled to herself. As bad as the situation was, at least she was in it with her brother.

"Jake?"

Her voice seemed to bounce off his shoulder as Jake was far too distracted by the thunder and lightning outside.

"Jake!"

This time, her voice stabbed him right between the shoulder blades.

Jake spun around. "Uh... what's up?"

"I was just wondering," Polly hesitated. "Do you have any idea what's happening?"

Jake pulled a face. "Not really, I was sort of leaving things to you!" A grin broke across his face. "You actually seem to know what you're doing... for once!"

Polly gave her brother a playful slap.

"So where did you get them, you know, the bubbles?"

"Off the old man... I mean, the King."

"The King in the hat?"

Polly nodded. "He exchanged them for £2.50."

"Exchanged? Don't you mean you bought them?"

"I don't think I was given much choice as far as I can remember. One minute he was there and the next he wasn't!"

"Like at the bedroom door," said Jake.

"Pretty much," replied Polly. She began to tell Jake the whole story of everything that had happened after the old man had given her the Magic Bubbles. How, she and Marcia had been transported in a giant bubble through a rainbow to the mysterious and enchanting Dizzelwood, only narrowly escaping being 'popped' by Sor-Ben-Rez disguised as a bird. Jake was enthralled as Polly told how the Forest Queen had sent them on a quest to rescue the King, who had been kidnapped by the evil Sor-Ben-Rez, who used to serve as the Royal High Counsel before becoming their sworn enemy.

Polly trembled and shivered as she related and relived the events of the Tree of Darkness, with its enormous hollow trunk filled with hundreds of dead stick people. It was here that they'd had their second encounter with Sor-Ben-Rez, this time disguised as a monstrous spider.

Then, after some perilous navigating through masses of deadly tree roots, they found themselves again face to face with Sor-Ben-Rez, along with the captured King. After a nasty battle (which they had so nearly lost), Polly and Marcia had managed to trap and vanquish the evil stick man in a magical double-bubbled-fireball, which they'd hoped would put an end to him once and for all.

After releasing the King, Polly told Jake how she had used the **Magic Bubbles** to restore Dizzelwood to its former glory before coming back home. Jake listened to the whole story mostly in silence, taking everything in and only interrupting with the odd question if he didn't understand something she had said.

"I didn't mean to keep it a secret... I just somehow forgot. I don't know how I could've possibly forgotten, I just did!"

Jake looked at his sister thoughtfully as he weighed everything up. "It's all right, sis, you always were a bit of a scatter-brain!" They both laughed. "Look, you've even knocked poor Marcia out with your smelly armpits!" Somehow in all the chaos, Marcia had fallen fast asleep. Jake leant over to ruffle Polly's hair. "You're a good friend, Pol, and..."

"And what?" Polly waited for the sting in the tail.

"And not a bad sister too!" grinned Jake.

"I wish I could say the same for you!"

Jake's grin faded to a shocked look. Polly couldn't help laughing.

"Cheeky, I'm going to tell Mum and Dad on you!"

The mention of Mum and Dad brought everything back into sharp focus. The horrible thought of both their parents and younger brother cocooned beneath sticky cobwebs wiped the smiles off their faces.

"Jake, what are we going to do?"

"I don't know, Pol, but I'm sure we'll figure something out."

Dusk was falling as the bubble started to descend rapidly.

"*Whoa!* What's happening?" screamed Jake in a squeaky high pitched voice.

Polly was the first to notice. "The outer bubble's gone."

Jake stared in disbelief. "I didn't hear it pop. Did you hear it pop?" he asked, his normal voice fully restored.

The single-skinned bubble continued to plummet earthwards in a most un-bubble-like fashion.

Marcia awoke, eyes bulging and her long frizzy curls shooting upwards. Polly rose to her feet, rubbing her bandaged hand.

"Maybe you should blow another bubble?" suggested Jake, hopefully.

"I don't think that's going to help."

Marcia was scribbling, her panicky scrawl in big capitals barely legible:

"Marcia, if you can't say anything to help, then please don't say anything at all!" snapped Polly, sounding much too much like her mother.

The ground was hurtling towards them, getting closer and closer like a giant darkening canvas eager to extinguish them.

THINK, POLLY, THINK!

Polly reached into her pocket. It took all her strength to pull the tiny bottle free and when she did, she was straining to hold on to it, even in two hands.

"It's the bubbles, they're dragging us downwards!"

The distance between them and the ground was diminishing at an alarming rate, their earthly impact now just seconds away.

"Let them go, Pol!"

Polly glared.

She couldn't,
she just cou—

*"Pol, let them
go! NOW!"*

Polly opened
her fingers, the
bubble container
plunging straight
through the
bubble's surface.

Instantly, the bubble resumed its floaty lightness, now drifting gently downwards. But the nightmare was far from over, as below them the ground yawned open in the gathering gloom.

"It's a giant hole," breathed Jake.

And so it was – a hole that Polly was sure wasn't there moments before.

Could this have something to do with the Magic Bubbles?

Regardless, their bubble was being drawn towards the vast muddy hole, threatening to gobble them whole as they entered the

dark depths deep deep below ground.

Chapter Six

Into the Mud

The devouring darkness swallowed them up instantly as the bubble descended

down down forever down...

Gloops of mud splattered all over the bubble's surface, slowly coating it in a brown sloopy goo that slithered and slimed everywhere. Miraculously, the bubble's surface held, although in places, the nasty slime started to ooze through, much to Marcia's disgust as she frantically scribbled something in the darkness and rapped her slate.

"It's no good writing, Marcia, we can't see a thing!"

If Marcia could have scribbled a sigh, she most certainly would have. Instead, there was just silence – the most silent silence that any of them could ever have imagined.

Down down forever down...

The bubble, now completely covered in oozy-gloopy mud, continued its descent with more and more of the muddy gunky-goo sliming its way through the bubble's surface. The mud was now running down the inside, forming ever deeper muddy puddles, with the three companions getting splattered in complete muddy blackness.

"I don't suppose this happened to you before?" asked Jake.

Polly shook her head, invisible in the black.

"I didn't think so," replied Jake, somehow sensing her movement rather than seeing it.

Down
down
forever
down...

The bubble seemed to be levelling out, at least that's what the sinking feeling in their tummies indicated. They were travelling mostly horizontally, occasionally punctuated by a sudden rise or dip, rather than plummeting further downwards. Whether this was a good or a bad thing was anyone's guess, although it was definitely less distressing.

Time passed slowly, the gloopy mud around Polly's feet slowly and steadily rising, along with the sense of panic that she was feeling deep inside. Polly didn't know what to do – she felt that if she opened her mouth she might scream so loudly that its intensity might burst their fragile bubble. Yet as long as the darkness continued and the sloopy mud got deeper and deeper (now creeping up her legs), the more likely it was that she would let out a bubble-bursting scream! She briefly thought of moving closer to the bubble side to escape the gloop, but when she reached out she could feel muddy slime running freely through her fingers on the inside of the bubble.

The scream grew inside her like a sonic bubble of dread longing to escape from her body – to escape and never stop running. Just when she thought she could stand no more, Polly saw it.

A light, glowing faintly at first, but steadily growing in intensity shone like a beacon of hope.

The muddy bubble bobbed and weaved its way through an invisible tunnel drawn towards the light as though to a strange magnet.

"It's the Bubbles!" exclaimed Jake.

Her brother was right. The light was coming from the golden top, which shone like a miniature sun amidst the muddy gloom.

How did it get there?

"How on earth did it get here?" said Jake, echoing his sister's thoughts.

POP!

The bubble disintegrated, plonking the three mud-splattered companions onto the soft muddy earth.

Marcia let out a barely audible groan which could only be translated as "Yuck!"

Polly trudged through the mud to retrieve the small glowing container. She noticed that Marcia's makeshift bandage had vanished, but in the greater scheme of things, it didn't really matter.

Releasing the bubble container from the mud, she held it in her hand like a torch, the eerie glow of the

Magic illuminating the tunnel.

Marcia and Jake were splattered with mud, with Marcia looking particularly distressed at her muddy appearance.

Polly felt an icy chill coursing through her. Memories of her and Marcia's journey through the dreaded Tree of Darkness flooded back like an unwelcome torrent of horribleness. This time there were no spiders or dead stick people covered with cobwebs, and instead of the chill of the Tree, the tunnel was surprisingly warm.

Polly closed her eyes, letting the muddy warmth evaporate the icy dread of bad memories. "We're safe," she said, not really knowing how she knew that for a fact. "Follow me."

The three plodded through the gloopy mud along the never-ending tunnel, encompassed by the reassuring glow of the Magic. The only sound that could be heard was the

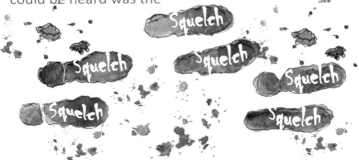

as each of their footsteps were met with sticky resistance. Polly's legs were beginning to tire, but with no place for them to sit and rest, she plodded on against the aching of her muscles. Thankfully, the tunnel began to widen, getting ever bigger, until finally they found themselves in a large elongated cavernous tunnel.

"*Wow!*" breathed Jake, "I've never seen anything like this!"

"I wouldn't get too excited," began Polly, "this is normally the time where things start to go wro—"

At that moment, the mud started to bubble and boil all around them.

Polly was about to shout *'RUN!'* but with nowhere obvious to run to.

Marcia wrapped her arms around Polly's waist as if her life depended on it as Polly reached out for her brother's hand.

"We're sinking!" cried Jake, his panic-edged voice echoing around the cavern tunnel.

"No," replied Polly. "Look!"

Masses of muddy mounds began to extrude themselves upwards from the slime, like mucky stalagmites. Slowly, the muddy extrusions began to bulge, growing limbs as they transformed into human-like figures, a little taller than Polly and about the same height as Jake.

"Here we go again," muttered Polly.

Jake stared at her wide-eyed. "You mean you've seen this before?"

"Not quite," replied Polly, "they were more like—"

"Stick people," said a voice, low and almost fluid like.

Jake's eyes almost popped out of his head!

"I see you have the Magic," continued the still transforming pile of mud closest to them; its face the last to form.

Polly closed her hand securely around the small container, its glowing light streaming through the gaps in her fingers. The mud man waved his arm in a wide arc – moments later, light flooded the tunnel cavern,

78

illuminating dozens of similar mud men, although not quite as tall.

"Who are you and what do you want?" demanded Polly, with a braveness she didn't feel.

The mud man smiled. "Now, those are exactly the questions that I should be asking you," he said, "if I didn't already know the answers."

"You do?"

Another smile. "Yes, at least, mostly."

"Are you anything to do with the spiders?" blurted Jake.

The mud man regarded Polly's brother carefully before answering.

"Spiders, no, those foul arachnids fortunately are not too fond of our..." he paused as if searching for the correct word, "environment," he finished.

The mud man gestured towards the multitude of still-forming-and-as-of-yet-incomplete mud people.

"We have been waiting for you, although we did not expect your arrival so soon."

"How did you know we were coming?" challenged Polly.

"Why, the King of course!"

"The King? The King was here?"

The mud man offered a slow shake of the head, as if anything faster might cause it to fall off.

"The King seldom visits the Under Earth, but he has been in communication."

"And how do we know that we can trust and believe you?" questioned Polly, feeling braver with each passing second.

The mud man's appearance began to change, becoming taller and bigger. The mud began **sliming** and **blooping** and **blopping** as he slowly re-transformed into an exact muddy replica of the King himself, complete with his crooked top hat!

"Wow!" breathed Jake.

Moments later, the mud began to topple and slide, until the mud man was back to his usual self. He smiled, although whether this was a smile of triumph or not, it was difficult to tell.

"What about Sor-Ben-Rez?" continued Polly, unconvinced by his muddy performance.

The mud man stopped smiling. "The Rogue is not welcome here, and his name should not be spoken, lest he discover your whereabouts sooner than he ought. But, in answer to your question, the Rogue is after the Magic."

"Tell me something I don't know."

"Indeed I will," replied the mud man, ignoring Polly's sarcastic tone. "The Rogue is after the Magic and has sent his envoys to draw you into a trap."

"Envoys?" queried Jake.

"Spiders," said Polly, impatient to hear more, whilst at the same time dreading what the mud man might say.

"Indeed, the Rogue is currently hiding out at some hidden location. All we know is that it's not far away and closer than we would like — either above or below the earth."

"That's helpful," remarked Jake.

"I am being helpful," insisted the mud man, casting Jake a reprimanding look. "It seems as though we are

81

forgetting our manners. I am Floo-yah, Regent of the Under Earth. I know of Pollyanna and her friend, Marcia, but you, my friend, remain something of a mystery."

"I'm Jake," said Jake, "Polly's older brother."

"A reader," observed Floo-yah.

"How did you know that?" asked Jake, astounded.

"I see it," replied the mud Prince, flatly.

"But—"

Floo-yah's form once again began to change, this time into an exact muddy replica of Jake. Jake stood open mouthed, unable to speak as he took in his mud-murky reflection. Seconds later, Floo-yah re-transformed himself back to his usual appearance.

"We will need your wisdom at a critical point in the future."

Polly had to stifle a giggle at the absurdity of Floo-yah's statement, but her humour evaporated when she saw the serious look on the mud Prince's face.

"You have the Magic, Pollyanna, and your brother may well have the knowledge. You will need both in order to defeat the Rogue."

Marcia started to scribble.

"You too, young Marcia. You have your own responsibilities and talents to add."

Marcia managed something of a smile, more than happy to be able to contribute something, although the thought of meeting Sor-Ben-Rez again filled her with dread.

The mud Prince stared at Marcia for long moments, his head slightly cocked. Then reaching out his hand, his arm elongated,

s–t–r–e–t–c–h–i–n–g

longer and longer

his fingers reaching for Marcia's throat.

Polly sprang into action, striking down hard to knock Floo-yah's arm away, her forearm and wrist passing straight through the mud arm, leaving it unaffected.

Marcia emitted a muffled squeal as Floo-yah's muddy fingers wrapped around the startled girl's neck.

"That's enough, mud face!" Jake threw himself at Floo-yah trying to knock him over, but just like Polly moments before, he passed straight through; the mud Prince's semi-fluid body without any effect.

Marcia's muffled squeal rose to a scream, getting louder and louder; then, suddenly, she stopped.

Floo-yah removed his fingers and his elongated arm retracted back to its normal size. Marcia rubbed her neck and throat.

"*I can speak!*" she said.

Floo-yah smiled. "Now, you are all fully equipped as you should be." The mud Prince thought for a moment.

"No, not quite..." Floo-yah's arm lengthened again, now reaching down into the mud's hidden depths, as if searching for something. "Ah, here it is!" he reached out towards Marcia. "A present to use against the Rogue should you need to."

In his hand was a small oval box made of what looked like hardened mud.

"What is it?" asked Marcia.

"Part of our Kingdom," replied Floo-yah, "you may find it useful against the Rogue – but do not open it until you're sure."

"Sure of what?" asked Marcia.

"You will know when the time comes. In the meantime, keep it safe and well hidden."

With a grateful nod, Marcia tucked the mud box safely away. "I was wondering," she began, not sure how to phrase her request, "if you could do something about the mud."

"This is the Under Earth," said Floo-yah, matter of factly.

"And these used to be my best pink top and leggings," countered Marcia, looking disgustedly at her mud-stained garments.

"Oh, I see," observed Floo-yah, lifting a hand. From somewhere up above, three waterfalls cascaded down onto the unsuspecting companions, drenching them clean of all traces of mud in seconds.

The deluge over, Marcia shivered in barely concealed contempt, glaring at the mud Prince and about to tell him in no uncertain terms what she thought of her impromptu shower.

Floo-yah held up a restraining hand, stopping the sodden girl in her tracks. Then, bringing his hand sharply down, there was a rumble from beneath their feet. Before any of them could move, Polly, Jake and Marcia were blasted off the ground by plumes of drying hot air.

Bathing in the soothing stream several feet above the ground, Polly and Jake relished the experience, while Marcia struggled to keep her top down to maintain something of her dignity. All too soon, the hot air plumes ceased, the three companions now lowered gently to the ground, completely dry again.

"The Rogue is on the move. He threatens not only this Kingdom, but many others also so be on your guard!"

Floo-yah's voice rose to a crescendo, filling the entire cavern.

"Things above and things below sometimes come together."

With these words, Floo-yah and the rest of the mud people began to dissolve, losing their form as they collectively sank lower and lower, once again becoming part of the muddy ground.

"Wait!" cried Polly. "What about my parents?"

Floo-yah's voice returned to normal. "You will be escorted safely above. Remember, you have the Magic...."

"But—"

"...and the Power of Three." Floo-yah dissolved into the mud, along with all the other mud people, leaving the three companions on their own.

"Great," sighed Polly, "more silly riddles and now it's just us again! Why can't they ever—"

The mud began to ripple and surge, first as small waves, then getting

Bigger and BIGGER!

The three companions found themselves being carried along, cresting their mud waves like expert surfers. **Faster** and **faster**, the mud waves surged forwards through the tunnel cavern, which split into a myriad of smaller tunnels separating the companions. Polly could hear Marcia's distant screams through the mud walls. She couldn't hear Jake, but then he was never one for making much noise anyway; if anything, her brother was probably enjoying the ride!

On and on they surfed the mud waves, sometimes speeding up and sometimes slowing down through tunnel after tunnel.

Suddenly, they were rising sharply upwards, no longer surfing but atop a fountain of mud!

Faster and **faster** and **faster**... until they found themselves spurted back out above ground.

Jake was already scrambling to his feet in the gloom as Polly broke through to the surface.

"You okay, sis?" he asked with a grin.

Polly nodded. "I'm fine, but where's Mar—?"

An echo-ey whoop, getting louder and louder, like the sound of an approaching police car as Marcia erupted to the surface in a fountain of mud!

"That was amazing!" she beamed, smoothing down her top as both Polly and Jake looked on in stunned silence.

From his secret hiding place, Sor-Ben-Rez desperately scanned the depths of the Crystal. He had been tracking them perfectly, even through the interference of the storm. Then suddenly, they had vanished!

He cursed himself for being so careless. Sor-Ben-Rez refocused and concentrated hard as he peered into the Crystal.

He would have to re-double his efforts, but find them he would, and when he did, the Magic would be his, once and for all...

Chapter Seven

SPIDER SNAKE

Somewhat surprisingly, they weren't caked in mud.

"It's good to have my voice back!" chirped Marcia.

"I'm surprised you haven't lost it again with all that screaming you were doing," retorted Jake.

"Screaming?" Marcia thought for a bit. "Oh that," she held up her hands, dismissing the absurd suggestion. "That wasn't screaming, that was fun!" she said eagerly rubbing her hands together. "So, what's next?"

Polly studied their misty surroundings; it was just starting to get light. *Had they been underground all that time?* She glanced across at Jake, who she guessed was thinking much the same thoughts.

More to the point, if it was so important to defeat Sor-Ben-Rez, why didn't Floo-yah offer more help? Even more infuriatingly, the mud Prince had totally ignored her plea for help in releasing her parents.

Polly sighed. "Do you have the mud box?"

Marcia nodded. "Safely hidden away."

"Well, make sure it stays safe – we're going to need all the help we can get if we're going up against Sor-Ben-Nasty."

Marcia managed a small smile, although she paled slightly at the Rogue's name.

Polly turned to her brother. "I don't suppose you've got any ideas?"

Jake shrugged. "Not yet, sis, you're the one with the Magic."

Her brother was right, the bubbles belonged to her. Then she half-remembered something.

Weren't the bubbles limited?

Polly needed to check the crumpled note that the bubbles had been wrapped in. She fished about in her pockets but it wasn't there.

It was either twelve or thirteen, but how many had she already used?

The fog in her mind was like the mist surrounding them so she would have to make a guess of maybe four or five bubbles, leaving only seven or eight bubbles left.

If only she could be sure!

"Jake, Marcia, how many bubbles have we used?"

"Does it matter?" asked Jake.

Polly gave him her best 'I-wouldn't-be-asking-you-if-it-didn't-matter' glare.

"I don't know, maybe two or three," guessed Jake.

"Marcia?"

Her best friend shrugged. "Sorry, I'd lost my voice."

"What's losing your voice got to do with counting bubbles?"

"*I was ill!* If it was so easy, why didn't you count them?"

Marcia was right, Polly should have counted them herself. They were her bubbles and her responsibility. She would definitely count them from now on.

Polly winced in pain as the spider bite started to sting; a burning sensation increasing in the back of her hand.

"The spiders are coming! Quick, take cover!" Polly could see that Jake was about to ask one of his stupid and unnecessary questions. *"Now!"* she urged.

They scrambled behind a nearby bush. Then they waited... and waited... and waited some more.

The inevitable question came. "Are you sure about the spiders?" whispered Jake, more than a little loudly.

"Yes!" hissed Polly. "Now be quiet."

They waited again. They waited... and waited... and waited...

"Polly," this time it was Marcia, "are you su—"

Polly shot Marcia one of her best 'Of-course-I'm-sure-now-be-quiet!' looks.

"Just asking," whimpered Marcia, shrinking away.

They waited... and waited... and waited...

Polly was getting restless. Maybe the spiders weren't coming after all. Maybe she *had* got it wrong. Maybe... her right hand throbbed mightily; it was all she could do not to cry out.

"Look!" whispered Jake.

The two girls looked to where Jake was pointing. An army of spiders were approaching.

"You were right!" squeaked Marcia.

Polly felt sick, her injured hand smarting more and more, the closer and closer the spiders came.

"Are you all right?" enquired Marcia.

Polly managed a thin smile and a nod despite the increasing pain.

"I've got some more lip balm, if that helps?"

Polly screwed her eyes shut and shook her head; it was all she could do not to cry out in pain.

Thousands of spiders were marching in a writhing, winding arachnid snake, stretching to well over one hundred metres.

"What's that?" whispered Marcia.

Something was being carried in the middle section of the spider snake, instantly recognisable despite it being smothered in cobwebs.

"It's Dad's pipe!" gasped Jake. "What on earth are they doing with—"

Polly dug her brother in the ribs to stop his rising voice attracting any unwanted attention. Not a moment too soon, the snaking trail of spiders tramped out of sight. The pain in Polly's hand eased.

Jake tapped her on the shoulder. "Well done, sis! If you hadn't spotted them spiders we'd have been done for!"

Marcia rested a hand on Polly's arm. "It's the bite, isn't it?"

Tears streamed down Polly's face.

Marcia smiled. "Thank you for being so brave!"

"We have to go after them," said Polly through her tears, gathering up every ounce of resolve she had.

"What?" Marcia's smile vanished. *"Are you crazy?"*

"They've got Dad's pipe."

"It's only a pipe, Pol."

"I know it's only a pipe, but it's *Dad's pipe* and I think that somehow the bubbles and the pipe must be connected."

Jake shook his head, unsure of his sister's logic.

"Look, do you want to rescue Mum and Dad, or not? Because we're going after those spiders." Polly thrust her still stinging hand into her pocket, gripping the small bubble container reassuringly.

They crept along in silence, being careful to keep just the very tail of the spider-snake in sight. Polly's hand continued to throb achingly, but she knew they had to carry on. The spiders wound and snaked through the thick trees, oblivious to the fact that they were being followed as they headed towards their secret destination.

By now, dawn had fully broken, yet a mist still lingered high in the trees, leaving the air damp and chilled. The sound of birdsong echoed from somewhere above the mists, the birds happily basking in the warmth of the morning sun.

"They're splitting up," said Jake, as the tail section of the spider-snake veered off sharply to the right.

"It's just the tail," observed Polly. "We need to stay with the main group carrying Dad's pipe."

The three companions stopped until the departing tail segment was out of sight. Once it was safe, they continued at a brisk pace until they caught up with the main body of the spider-snake, all the while being careful to stay out of sight. On and on they marched beneath the lingering mist, the pain in Polly's hand subsiding a little to provide some welcome relief.

"Pol, something's wrong."

Polly kept marching, her eyes fixed on the remnant of the spider-snake.

"It's the mist," continued Jake, "it's beginning to thicken." Polly still didn't acknowledge him. "The sun must be quite high in the sky by now."

What on earth was Jake going on about?

"The birds have stopped singing too," persisted Jake. "Surely the mist should begin to burn away by now..."

Polly stomped on, increasing her pace to keep up with the spider-snake that was rapidly vanishing in the thickening fog.

"Pol, look out!"

TOO LATE!

Her spider bite flared, the pain agonising.

Polly almost collided into the rear of the spider-snake. They had been waiting for her in the thick fog just around the bend! Polly turned to run, but she was surrounded – the departed rear troop had circled around from behind!

"JAKE!"

The pain in her hand intensified as a huge spider web fell from above.

Polly lost consciousness.

The old man wasn't smiling. In fact, his face was grave and his normally twinkling blue eyes a sea of concern.

"Well, young lady, it looks like we've got ourselves into a right pickle!"

Polly looked around. Jake and Marcia were nowhere to be seen. Neither were the army of spiders.

"Where am I?"

"You're with me," said the King, "or rather, I'm with you!" For the first time, the old man managed a smile, although it wasn't a happy one. "I'm in your head and you're fast asleep. Don't worry, your friends are all right, at least for now, but there are dire dealings afoot."

Polly simply nodded, unsure of what else to do.

"They're after **the Mechanism**, or what you know as your Dad's pipe. Not only that, they're after you too, young lady. They're taking you to their Master, and he, as you well know, is a rather unpleasant character who's bent on exacting his revenge. Revenge on me..." the King looked at her earnestly, "...and revenge on you."

"But what's all this got to do with Dad's pipe?"

"I think you already know the answer to that question, Pollyanna."

"I do?"

The old man nodded. "What matters now is that we have a rescue plan. Now that he has **the Mechanism** in his grasp, it's absolutely imperative, my dear, that Sor-Ben-Rez does not get hold of **the Magic**. Under any circumstances whatsoever; absolutely not, or we will find ourselves in the direst of predicaments." The old man's face was grey and very, very serious. "It's not just Dizzelwood this time, as I am sure you're already aware. If the two come together, he will be unstoppable – absolutely and utterly and completely unstoppable! Do you understand?"

The King bent in close, their noses almost touching, his blue eyes filling her vision. Whether she understood or not, she knew that anything to do with Sor-Ben-Rez was Bad News. Images of her cobweb-covered parents and little brother once again flooded her mind.

"The Queen has sent some help, and I will do whatever I can, but time, my dear, is running out. The two must not come together, and yet as you already know, **things above and things below sometimes come together.**"

The old man started to fade.

"Wait! What does that mean?"

The old King was almost gone.

"You have all the answers you need..."

Chapter Eight

HOSTAGES!

Polly opened her eyes, her hand stinging like crazy.

Looking skywards at the misty tree tops, she was being caterpillared along the ground on the backs of thousands of spiders!

Polly tried to move but she was cocooned in a blanket of sticky webbing wound from her feet all the way up to her neck. Familiar feelings of panic started to rise up inside her – she needed to focus. Closing her eyes, Polly took a deep breath and did her best to relax. Then, using all her strength she flexed every muscle in an attempt to break free.

The webs held firm.

Distant memories crawled their way into her consciousness – frightful images of Sor-Ben-Rez and of her being trapped and helpless, threatened to overwhelm her as her tummy filled with wriggling worms of dread.

Polly needed help. She craned her neck as much as she could to look down the spidery snake. An unconscious Marcia lay up ahead cocooned on the snaking spidery conveyor belt.

"MARCIA?" hissed Polly as loud as she dared.

Marcia was out cold – she must have fainted! Polly briefly wondered if maybe the old man had appeared to Marcia too, but somehow she doubted it.

The King had said that she had all the answers she needed, but Polly knew as well as she knew anything that she didn't have any answers at all!

Why and how this was happening was a mystery.

Yes, she had the Magic Bubbles but in all honesty, she had never really wanted them in the first place – the King had just shoved them on her and taking all her money in the process!

One thing she did know – these bubbles were trouble, and if the old King was right, even BIGGER TROUBLE was lurking just around the corner, especially if that horrible Sor-Ben-

103

Rez got hold of the bubbles and her Dad's pipe...

AARRGGHHH!

Why didn't she ask the King how many bubbles she had left? And why did he always have to show up and then vanish again before Polly could get some answers?

What else was it the King had said?

Something about the Queen sending help. Well, now would be a good time for a rescue, before the spiders reached their destination, which could only mean one thing: Sor-Ben-Rez.

The thought of encountering the maliciously evil ex-Royal Advisor made the wriggly worms of dread in her stomach wriggle even more!

There was something else.

Something familiar.

Something she'd heard somewhere before.

'The two must not come together.'

No, that wasn't it; it was something else.

'Things above and things below sometimes come together.'

That was it! But what did it mean, and where had she heard it before?

The answer pierced the fog of her mind like an arrow: it was Floo-yah, the Mud Prince!

Polly was sure that he'd said the same thing; or did he? Doubt started to rattle and shake her convictions. Jake would know – her brother had a knack for remembering things, particularly odd things – normally the odder the better.

Where was Jake?

He'd been there at the ambush, of that she was certain. Polly wriggled, trying to move herself into a better position to see more. There was only Marcia. Polly manoeuvred again, stretching and turning as much as she could to try and get a better view, but as far as she could see, there was no sign of Jake anywhere.

What had the spiders done to her brother?

Could Jake have somehow managed to escape?

Polly cast her mind back. There was no way that he could have escaped, *so where was he?*

Why did she have to pass out?

Jake would never leave her, of that she was sure. But then, in that case, it meant that the spiders must have done something to him, which didn't bear thinking about.

"MARCIA?" Polly hissed again, this time louder.

Marcia twitched but stayed unconscious.

Polly bit her lip in frustration – she would have to wait. In her current situation she was helpless to do anything anyway. If something bad had happened to Jake, then she would know – deep down inside, she would definitely know.

Polly forced her thoughts on to other matters. Wriggling her fingers, she probed the outside of her pocket. A familiar lump bulged – at least the bubbles were still in her possession. Her hand, although still painful was more of a throb than a stabbing sting.

The thought of riding on a trail of arachnids was hideous, particularly as they were also in her hair. At least the ride was smooth for the most part, except when they had to traverse a fallen tree, then the spider-snake would arch, bending her back painfully with it. With every rise, Polly could see Marcia (still unconscious), on the snaking line of spiders ahead.

Polly would have to wait for her best friend to wake, and maybe then she could get some answers.

Jake stared at the four small men in disbelief, relieved at least to be away from the spiders. He was not completely sure what had happened. One minute they were following the end of the spider trail, the next, they were surrounded, and he was being hauled upwards!

Now they were all sitting up in a tree.

One of the men held a finger to his lips. "Not a sound, we're here to rescue you."

A fourth man just behind him released his hand from Jake's mouth.

"Who are you?"

"Friends."

"How do I know I—"

"Pollyanna."

"You know Pol?"

The four men nodded in unison.

"Pollyanna's the reason we're here. We're her friends. My name's Izz and these are my brothers, Ozz, Igg and Ogg. And you're Master Jake."

"Thanks for the reminder. So where's my sister?"

"She was caught under the web before we could reach her," said Ozz.

"And Miss Marcia fainted," added Igg as his brothers nodded their vigorous agreement.

"Sounds about right," sighed Jake.

"No, no, it's not right at all. We were sent to rescue all of you – not just you!"

"No need to sound so disappointed," said Jake, rebalancing himself on the branch.

"We were sent by the King," said Ogg.

"The one in the hat?"

The brothers nodded.

"It's all gone a bit wrong," admitted Izz.

"So what's the back-up plan?" Jake's question was met by four clueless stares. "Are you saying that there's no back-up plan?"

Four nods.

"Great!"

"They're taking her to Sor-Ben-Rez," continued Izz.

"Tell me something I don't know."

Izz looked confused. "I'm afraid I don't know anything about what you don't know."

Jake sighed. "Do you know where they're heading?"

"Sor-Ben-Rez," offered Ogg.

"I know that – do you know his geographical location?"

The brothers looked blank.

"Do you know where he is?"

"We were hoping to rescue you before you got there."

"I guess that's a 'No' then."

"Yes."

Jake sighed again. "Looks like we're going to have to try a re-rescue."

"Great," said Izz brightening, "do you have a plan?"

"No," admitted Jake, "at least not yet. But one thing's for sure, nothing much is going to happen while we're stuck up in this tree."

Jake's first tentative attempts at finding the best way down without falling out of the tree altogether were taken completely out of his hands by Izz, who gripping him around the wrists, launched himself downwards. Jake let out a startled yelp before realising that he was now dangling inches about the ground, suspended by a chain of four brothers hanging down out of the tree canopy.

They were stronger than they looked!

Seconds later, everyone was safely on the ground. The four brothers stared at him expectantly.

Jake took a moment to get his bearings. "This way."

They set off, Jake leading with the four brothers trailing behind. Jake hoped that Polly and Marcia were all right, figuring that they should be, at least until they got to Sor-Ben-Rez's secret hiding place.

Jake's mind was turning over and over, trying to formulate some sort of plan. "Do we have any reinforcements?"

Izz looked at him quizzically.

"More people like you," added Jake.

"Oh yes."

"Where are they?"

The four brothers pointed at themselves in unison.

"Just you?"

Four nods.

"Great," groaned Jake.

At first, Polly didn't realise that they were slowing. It was only when Marcia was marched alongside that the whole spider-snake came to a complete stop.

"Have we stopped?" asked Marcia, finally awake.

"Marcia, where's Jake?"

"Jake?"

"Yes, did you see where they've taken him?"

"Who?"

"The spiders."

"The spiders have taken Jake?"

"I don't know – that's what I'm trying to figure out!"

"Sorry, I sort of fainted."

"It doesn't matter. Did you have any dreams?"

Marcia screwed up her face. "Yes, lots of them – all yucky and filled with awful, awful spiders!"

"Anything else?" asked Polly hopefully.

"Yes," replied Marcia thoughtfully. "Yes, there was something... now what was it?" Long seconds passed. "No, sorry, I can't remember."

"What about the King?" prompted Polly.

"The King?" Marcia brightened. "Is he here?"

"No, in your dream. Did you dream about the King?"

"Dream about the King? Why would I dream about a King? Now, if there was a handsome prince, that would be worth dreaming about, but—"

"Oh, never mind," groaned Polly.

They were lost.

They'd only been marching a matter of minutes and all Jake had successfully managed to do was to get them lost.

Hopelessly lost.

Jake hoped he wasn't giving anything away about how lost they were, but he knew the truth of it deep in his stomach.

They were lost – very, very lost.

Jake stopped to assess the situation. Trees crowded in from everywhere, and everywhere looked the same. With no spider tracks or tell-tale spider web strands to follow, things were not looking good. He needed to find Polly and Marcia – that was all that mattered.

Think, Jake, think!

"Master Jake?"

It was Ozz.

"We were wondering..." Ozz shifted a little uneasy.

"We were wondering..." echoed Igg, unable to finish.

"Where we were heading," finished Ogg.

Jake took a deep breath. It was time to confess. "We're—"

Gloop!

"Look!" Izz was pointing.

The ground just in front of Jake was beginning to bubble and pop, its hardness turning into liquid mud! Then, from the muddy mess emerged a spider...

a large muddy spider...

then another...

and another...

and another...

and another!

Five muddy giant spiders standing around the newly formed muddy pool.

Waiting.

Jake's thoughts flashed back to Floo-yah and the Underground Kingdom.

What was it the Mud Prince had said?

'Things above and things below sometimes come together.'

"They're here to help!"

The four brothers were not so sure, staring warily at the spiders before turning their attention back to him.

"Things above and things below sometimes come together," Jake said, hoping that they'd understand.

They didn't.

More uncertain looks from the wood folk, not sure if their impromptu leader had lost his mind as well as his sense of direction.

They needed more convincing.

Jake tentatively approached the nearest spider.

The mud spider clicked its mandibles, gloops of mud drip-drip-dripping from its semi-liquid body.

Jake wavered.

Before he lost his nerve completely, he lifted one gangly leg and spun on the other, seating himself firmly down on the spider's back. More gloops of mud splashed and sprayed, but otherwise, the mud spider remained intact. It felt very squidgy under Jake's bottom, but at least it wasn't damp.

Seeing that the mud spider bore Jake's weight did nothing to entice the brothers any closer, each one keeping his distance whilst observing silently. Jake briefly thought of maybe stroking the mud spider to demonstrate how tame and harmless it was, but just sitting on the giant arachnid was just about using up all of Jake's bravery reserves.

Having carefully weighed up their options, each of the brothers cautiously stepped forward, reluctantly selecting their own arachnid. Then, in one synchronous motion, all four mounted simultaneously.

The mud spiders immediately started moving

downwards

sinking into the muddy earth!

Izz, Ozz, Igg and Ogg started to panic. Jake would have too, if not for his previous venture underground.

"Relax guys, it's all part of the plan," he said, hoping he sounded confident and that he wasn't inadvertently leading them into another trap.

All five mud spiders submerged beneath the earth with their nervous passengers still aboard. The spiders burrowed their way deep through the clay, although to the companions it seemed more like the ground itself was simply opening up before them. How it did this was beyond Jake's comprehension, but for once, he didn't care. Sometimes the spiders zig-zagged to avoid large boulders and the occasional small subterranean animal, peering curiously from their underground lairs as the unexpected travellers careered by, with one or more of the brothers offering their apologies as they did so.

Could the spiders be taking them back to Floo-yah, the Mud Prince?

Jake dismissed the notion instantly. What was the point? They would just be losing time. No, these mud spiders had been sent for a reason – to help rescue Polly and Marcia, and at the rate they were moving through the earth, it wouldn't be long before they caught up or even overtook them.

Suddenly, the spiders came to a stop.

Polly had an uncanny feeling they were being followed. How she knew this she didn't know – she simply knew. What's more, she knew something else too – it was Jake – the throbbing in her hand had subsided and in its place was a warm comforting heat.

Jake was close, and he was coming to rescue her!

Sor-Ben-Rez was seething!

Everything was going to plan, yet somehow, the boy had disappeared. He peered into the Crystal, probing with all his powers to detect the boy and his four cronies, but they had simply vanished...

The mud spiders were on the move again. For one awful moment Jake thought that they were completely lost and that they would be trapped deep beneath the earth forever. A quick glance at the brothers' faces revealed that they were having similar thoughts too.

Whatever it was, it didn't matter now. At least they were on the move again.

Maybe they were just getting their bearings...

The warmth in her hand faded like the sun caught behind an unwanted cloud. The throbbing ache returned, feeling much worse now that the warmth was gone. Wherever Jake was, he was no longer near, of that Polly was certain.

They were heading **deeper and deeper downwards**, each of the riders now having to lean back in order to keep their balance on the scurrying arachnids. The urgency of the mud spiders was unsettling as they continued at speed towards an unknown destination.

Chapter Nine

SPIDER'S LAIR

It seemed like an age before they exited the trees. The long spider-snake meandered into a clearing with a large lake at its centre, but this was no ordinary lake. There before them, instead of water was a sea of sticky spider webs!

Without breaking their stride, the spiders marched straight onto the lake's webby surface, which sagged threateningly under the weight of the spiders and their human cargo.

On and on the spiders tramped, with Marcia screaming and yelling about stupid spiders and that it would be safer for them to go around and not over the treacherous lagoon.

Polly kept silent, wondering what lay ahead. One thing she knew for sure: whatever it was, it wasn't going to be good.

Finally, the spider entourage arrived at the centre of the lake, its web-encrusted surface sagging and stretching seemingly to its limits, but fortunately, not breaking.

Then Marcia was off again, screaming even louder as the spiders began to descend through the webby surface, taking Marcia with them, head first.

"Polly, help! They're dragging me under!"

Polly struggled against her webby bonds, but it was no use. She looked on in horror as Marcia was dragged screaming beneath the surface, her cries muffled and then silenced completely as her best friend submerged into the hidden depths.

Polly's insides jingled and jangled in knots of twisted terror, but there was nothing she could do. Seconds later, she too was being pulled under the sea of webs. Polly tried desperately to retrieve the bubbles in her pocket, but it was no good.

Polly screwed her eyes shut and took a deep breath, hoping the end would be quick. The webs clung and slimed across her face as she was pulled down, deeper and deeper.

Polly was somehow being rotated through the sticky clinging mess until she was no longer upside-down. Images of her Mum, Dad and Joshy flitted through her mind, her head giddy and her lungs burning. Unable to hold on any longer, Polly knew that she had to take another breath. She opened her mouth and to her grateful surprise, she was able to breathe.

Polly gulped in the stale, putrid air, which although far from fresh, was at least breathable.

Polly was being winched down into a cavernous hole. Up above, she could see the webby strands of the underside of the lake, its under-surface showing no evidence of their passing through.

Marcia was gasping and squirming as she disgustedly spat out strands of sticky spider web.

Far, far below the ground was moving and alive with hundreds of thousands of swarming spiders! Polly just caught sight of her Dad's pipe before it vanished into the sea of arachnids.

The sides of the enormous cavern were steep, with ledges around its circumference, forming crude circular steps from top to the bottom. Countless spiders teemed down the sides, tumbling from one ledge to another in a gruesome black waterfall cascading to the bottom. Still more spiders were descending from above from strands suspended from the underside of the lake's surface.

Down...

Down...

Down...

The dank air clung to Polly's skin like wet cling film in the gloomy half-light. The swirling sea of spiders began to scatter, mercifully leaving her a small pool of spider-less space as her back touched down onto the cold rocky surface. The nasty swarming spiders jostled and shoved at each other, eyeing her with evil intent. Then suddenly, the arachnid army multitude began to disperse, rapidly deserting the web-topped cavern as if summoned by an invisible force.

Something else – or more accurately, lots and lots of something else's caught Polly's eye: from the lowermost ledge some twelve feet up, hung hundreds of sacs the size of large footballs, suspended by sticky cobwebs, their brown leathery surfaces jiggling and bulging menacingly. These things were alive, and whatever was inside was desperate to get out!

Polly pushed away her dark nagging thoughts to turn her attention to Marcia, who had somehow managed to pass out yet again!

"Marcia!"

Nothing.

"MARCIA!"

Still nothing.

"MAR—"

Polly's hand started to prickle, not a painful tingle but warm and reassuring one.

"Jake?" Polly looked around as best she could but there was no sign of her brother anywhere. All the while, her hand was getting warmer. "Jake, is that you?" Her brother could sometimes be a bit of a prankster, but surely—

"Hiya, Pol!"

Polly would have jumped out of her skin if she wasn't cocooned tightly in cobwebs.

Jake was kneeling next to her grinning from ear to ear like a Cheshire Cat.

"Where on earth did you come from?"

"Maybe *'Where in earth?'* would be a better question."

"What?"

"Keep still, sis, I'll have you free in a jiffy!" Jake proceeded to cut through her webby bonds with his penknife.

"But where did you—?"

"SSSHHHH! Questions later. Let's just get you out of here first!"

In a matter of seconds Polly was free, although her arms and legs felt stiff and heavy. She moved tentatively, allowing the strength to seep back into her body. Rising unsteadily to her feet, she staggered over to Jake who was busy cutting through Marcia's bonds.

Marcia awoke with a startled yelp.

"SSSHHHH!" they both hissed in unison.

Miraculously, Marcia managed to hold herself together until she was free, Polly helping her friend, who was a bit wobbly, back to her feet.

"How on earth did you get here?"

Jake grinned. "The same way we're getting out."

From the shadows crawled a large spider – a spider made completely of mud!

"You came on *that...*?" then Polly remembered. "Floo-yah!"

"Things above and things below sometimes come together." Both brother and sister recited the peculiar phrase together.

"Do you expect us all to travel on that?" asked Marcia, wrinkling her nose in disgust.

"Don't worry, we've got some more," grinned Jake, motioning with his hand.

Out of the ground emerged four more mud spiders, together with their riders.

"Izz, Ozz, Igg and Ogg!" Polly rushed to greet her old friends. "You came!"

"Yes mistress, we did, but not quite as we had anticipated," said Izz. "The Queen sent us to—"

"I know," said Polly, "the King told me."

Izz brightened immediately. "The King is here?"

"No," replied Polly, "he's in my head, or at least he was."

"Oh," sighed Izz, his three brothers echoing his disappointment in a collective trio of sighs.

"Do you still have it?" asked Ozz.

Polly thought for a moment. "Oh, you mean the Ma—"

"Yes!" cried the four brothers as one.

"Are they talking about the bubb—?" began Marcia.

"SSSHHHH!" shushed the brothers.

"There's far too much 'SSHHH-ing' going on, and not enough doing," urged Jake. "Let's get out of here!"

"But there's not enough spiders," bleated Marcia.

"I thought you weren't that keen?" retorted Jake, before his tone softened. "But you can travel with me if you like."

"Look!" Ozz was pointing at Jake's mud spider who appeared to be changing shape. No, not changing — dividing into two mud spiders — and again into three mud spiders!

"Ladies," Jake offered a mock bow, "your carriages await. Now, if you'd both like to climb aboard?"

Polly didn't need asking twice, quickly hopping astride her spider; Marcia however, hung back.

"Oh, come on, Marcia!" urged Polly.

Marcia took a few uneasy steps towards the waiting arachnid. The mud spider lowered itself slightly to allow her to get on.

Marcia pulled a face. "It's a bit icky!"

The other companions implored her to get a move on, until finally, Marcia obliged, albeit reluctantly.

With everyone safely aboard, the mud spiders began to make their escape. Suddenly, Marcia's spider exploded in a muddy mess. Marcia screamed.

The other mud spiders scurried faster, but it was too late – they too exploded in the same muddy fate.

"Leaving so soon?"

Polly recognised the crackly voice instantly.

"Well, well, well, what have we here? Looks like we have caught a number of flies in our trap!"

The hapless companions would have made a run for it, only their feet were now webbed securely to the ground.

A vast sea of spiders escorted Sor-Ben-Rez, seated on a throne of living spiders into the arena. The arachnid ocean came to a halt, parting to form a clear path as their insidious leader strode forward; the spider throne quickly dissolving back into the sea of spiders.

Unlike the rest of the stick people who had transformed back into their former human selves, Sor-Ben-Rez remained as sticklike as ever. His red-orange chest blazed in the half light, as merciless unblinking black pea eyes looked on in sinister amusement.

"It's been a long time. One might say almost too long." A twisted smile spread beneath his crookedy nose. "And I see this time you've brought me some more friends to meet. How kind! My spiderlings will enjoy feasting on their extra morsels." Sor-Ben-Rez stepped nearer, masses of spiders scurrying aside to make space for their leader. "I do hope you've brought a gift for us all." Sor-Ben-Rez reached out his stick arm and lifted his head in concentration. "Yes! Yes! I can feel the Magic! I have waited a long time for you, my dear." The smile vanished. ***"Now, give it to me!"***

A crescendo of spiders clicked menacingly, chanting in their own spider clicking language, the chorus growing

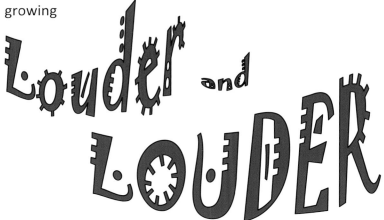

Louder and LOUDER

"Don't do it!" yelped Marcia.

Sor-Ben-Rez swung around, a ball of web shooting from his hand and securely gagging Marcia's mouth.

"You would be wise to maintain your silence!" Sor-Ben-Rez turned his attention back to Polly. "Now, the Magic – *Give it to me!*"

Polly reached into her pocket, wondering how quickly she could unscrew the top and blow a bubble. It was their only chance. With her fingers still deep inside her pocket, Polly slowly started to unscrew the top.

A gurgling cry echoed around the chamber.

IT WAS JAKE!

Webs were tightening around his neck. Her brother was beginning to choke.

"No tricks now, or he dies!"

Polly stopped unscrewing the top.

"Don't listen to him, Pol, he's going to kill us anywa—" The webs tightened again, Jake's face rapidly losing colour.

"Give me the Magic and I will release him!"

Polly tossed the container to the stick man.

"RELEASE MY BROTHER NOW!"

"Brave words, little one." Sor-Ben-Rez snapped his fingers. Immediately, the webbing around Jake's neck loosened.

"Jake, are you all right?" Her brother smiled, managing a nod. Polly turned steely eyed to face their captor. "You have **the Magic** so now you can release us!"

"And why would I do that?" sneered Sor-Ben-Rez.

"You wouldn't," countered Polly, "unless you were afraid."

Sor-Ben-Rez regarded her with cold unblinking eyes, assessing the situation. The crooked smile reappeared. "Me, afraid? I have all that I need, how can I possibly be afraid? Bring me **the Mechanism**!"

Moments later, a new horde of arachnids pushed through the spider masses carrying Dad's pipe.

'The two must not come together.'

The old man's voice boomed through Polly's mind, but even now she suspected it was too late.

"At last! At last!" crowed the stick man. "I have them both – the Mechanism and the Magic!" Sor-Ben-Rez laughed in triumph, his crackly cackles echoing around the walls of the vast cavern. Once again, a mass of spider clicking rose to a crescendo as the creepy arachnids celebrated with their Master. "We look forward to having you all for dinner, but first, we have work to do. Bring me the basket!"

From out of the depths of the spider sea, a large basket about two metres square made completely of spider webs emerged.

Sor-Ben-Rez unscrewed the gold top and blew through the blower with a rasping breath. A small bubble began to form, growing Bigger...

and BIGGER...

and BIGGER...

As the bubble floated above the basket, spider webs were cast and flung over the top, connecting the bubble and basket like a translucent hot air balloon.

Tossing away the blower top, Sor-Ben-Rez took the ornate pipe and ran his stick fingers along its stem, caressing it with his eyes closed in deep concentration as if trying to unlock the pipe's secrets. Sor-Ben-Rez grimaced in frustration, then delight as *CLICK!* the pipe stem came away from the bowl. Then, taking the unstoppered tiny bubble container, Sor-Ben-Rez slid it into the barrel of the stem.

With a deft twist, the former Head Counsel reassembled the pipe with the bubble container now inside. The dark wood of the pipe grew darker and darker, now almost completely black as Sor-Ben-Rez held the pipe to his lips and blew.

A bubble started to form.

A bubble unlike any they had ever seen before, growing **Bigger...**

and BIGGER...

and

BIGGER...

nd

BIGGER...

until the enormous bubble spanned the whole cavern.

"Inside, my spiders, inside!"

The underground amphitheatre drained in a massive spider exodus, as the swarming blackness pushed through the bubble's surface to enter inside, filling its transparent volume with a writhing blackness.

The three companions looked on helplessly at the dire spectacle unfolding before them.

The spider filled bubble began to rise, **higher and higher and higher...** its top now pressing against the sea of webs forming the underside of the lake above. Pushing and stretching against the webby surface, the colossal bubble began to break through, causing strands of sticky webs to rain down in torrents!

As the gigantic bubble continued to rise, Sor-Ben-Rez climbed into his spider web basket; his smaller bubble balloon rising alongside the huge spider bubble.

"Oh look, it's our new babies!" Sor-Ben-Rez gestured excitedly towards the cobweb covered football sacs, some of which were beginning to crack and split. One sac burst sending a number of tiny spiderlings tumbling to the ground. Momentarily dazed, the spiderlings righted themselves and started crawling, tentatively getting used to their newborn legs. Meanwhile, hundreds more of their spider siblings began to descend from their erupted spider sacs, hungrily in search of nourishment.

Sor-Ben-Rez grinned, his eyes alight with malicious glee. "I'm afraid we might have to call off our dinner engagement. Our precious babies are looking particularly hungry, but try not to be too disappointed, I'm sure they will enjoy having you for dinner!"

"The King will never let you get away with this! You'll never conquer Dizzelwood!"

"Dizzelwood?" snarled Sor-Ben-Rez in mock surprise. "The King can keep his precious Dizzelwood – it shall be the last place to fall when I take over this human-ridden country of yours, and then, the world!"

Chapter Ten

BOUNCE!

"**C**ome on, Pol, don't just stand there!" Jake tossed Polly his penknife, having already cut through his sticky bonds, and was on the move.

Meanwhile, high above, the enormous spider bubble had exited the cavern, with Sor-Ben-Rez now hovering above it, his web basket tethered to the top of the giant bubble with more sticky strands.

"He's going to release his nasty spiders all over the world!" cried Marcia.

"He's going to release his nasty spiders all over us first," exclaimed Polly, the first sac now completely ruptured, with baby spiders swarming all over its surface.

"Not if we have anything to do with it, he won't!" said Jake defiantly.

Marcia was white with fear as more and more of the spider sacs began to crack and split with sinister spider synchronicity, ready to release thousands of baby spider assassins.

Polly hacked though the webs around her feet as the synchronised spider hatching gathered momentum, with more and more of the sacs ripping apart. Polly could feel her panic rising as she hurriedly passed the knife to Izz. "We're stuck down here with no way out!"

"Don't fret, sis, cos we're getting out of here – route one!"

"Route one? There are no routes anywhere, let alone route one – whatever that is!"

Jake grinned as he took hold of some of the webs hanging off the large ledges around the sides of the cavern. "We're going to bungee our way out of here!" Yanking down hard, the web stretched and retracted like a giant elastic band lifting Jake off the ground.

"But what about those sacs?"

Marcia was pulling and tugging at her feet in desperation. "I don't want to be eaten!"

Having freed the last of his brothers, Izz rushed to her rescue.

"Hold still, mistress, we'll soon have you free!"

BOUNCE!

Marcia smiled her best 'I'm-not-having-a-nervous-breakdown' smile as Izz set to work.

Polly was scouring the gloom. Finally, she found what she was looking for. Picking up Sor-Ben-Rez's discarded bubble blower top, she put it safely in her pocket.

"What use is that?" asked Marcia.

"They're my bubbles," said Polly determinedly, "and I'm going to get them back! Now, let's get out of here."

"But the baby spiders!" protested Marcia.

"Will you shut up about those spiders!" Polly had had enough, her anger now eclipsing her fear.

Having successfully exited their spider sacs, thousands of ravenous spiderlings descended in search of food. Even worse, the cobwebs holding several of the hatching sacs simultaneously snapped, the pods exploding as they hit the ground, releasing over a thousand more starving spiders!

Jake grabbed a handful of dangling webs. "Let's get out of here. Everyone grab some webs and start pulling!"

Marcia and the four wood folk remained stock still, their eyes transfixed on the rapidly approaching spiders.

Polly tried her best to reassure her reluctant companions as the newly hatched spiders swarmed

141

ever closer. "It's okay, Jake reads lots of books!" Why her brother's reading habits should make everything okay was not entirely clear, but what was very clear was that time was running out – fast! "On the other hand, you could always stay here for lunch!" Polly seized a handful of webs and pulled, amazed at how easily she was launched off the ground as the webs stretched and contracted. After a few initial mini bounces to gain her confidence, and with Jake already on the first ledge some twelve feet up, Polly tied a loop of webbing around her foot. Then, taking a deep breath, she yanked down with all her might.

Polly was catapulted skywards. Unfortunately, in all the excitement, Polly hadn't given much thought of what to do once in the air, so she just clung desperately to her webby lifeline. Having reached the top of her bounce, and with her head just about level with the first ledge, Polly reached out to grab it... and missed! With no other way but down, Polly's stomach sank to her shoes. She closed her eyes and waited for the inevitable.

The inevitable never came as a hand grabbed her wrist and pulled her up to safety. Polly opened her eyes and threw herself into her grinning brother's arms. They held each other gratefully in silence.

"Er..." said Jake awkwardly, "I think maybe we should help the others."

They peered over the ledge. Down below, some of the spiderlings were already upon them, the four brothers doing their best to stamp out the growing tide which was increasing second by second.

"Come on!" urged Jake.

"She won't come!" screamed Ozz, his dancing feet squishing and squashing several spiders.

Marcia was stamping too. "I'm not bouncing myself anywhere, least of all, up there!"

"What if we pull you up?" offered Polly.

Marcia's feet were having to move faster and faster as she squished several more spiders.

"Mistress, we can help," Izz crouched as he cupped both hands.

Using his brother's hands as a step, Ozz climbed up and stood on Izz's shoulders. Next it was Igg's turn, clambering up on Ozz's shoulders; and finally Ogg, now as high as the ledge. Polly was reminded of her and Marcia's first encounter with the brothers as stick men, when three of the brothers had combined to make one giant stick man.

"Climb up, mistress!" urged Izz, under the growing strain of the combined weight of his brothers. "Don't worry, we won't let you go."

"I've got a dress on," protested Marcia, her dancing feet already beginning to tire.

Izz stared in confusion.

"It's not that good for climbing..." explained Marcia. "*I'm* not that good at climbing."

"Don't worry, mistress Marcia, we won't fail you."

With the brothers' help and lots of Marcia's squealings, she eventually clambered up to the safety of the ledge. Seconds later, she was joined by the brothers, frantically dusting off the scrambling spiders from their clothes, the dislodged spiderlings tumbling haplessly over the ledge.

"One down, lots more to go!" said Jake, almost too cheerfully.

Desperate for their lunch not to get away, the predatory spiderlings were already scaling the wall below them as more and more spider sacs began to explode in a cacophony of alarming 'POPS'! Both the wall and the ground beneath them were now alive with thousands of baby spiders, all in search of their escaping lunch.

With not a second to lose, the companions continued their journey steadily upwards, ledge by ledge; Polly and Marcia climbing up the Izz-Ozz-Igg-Ogg totem pole, while Jake bungeed happily from ledge to ledge.

They were making good progress when suddenly, Jake's web inexplicably detached itself from the ledge above. Arms flailing wildly, Jake tumbled downwards. Ogg lunged, managing to grab hold of him just in time. Unfortunately, Ogg then lost his footing, sending both of them sliding towards the edge! With the three brothers still forming a tower and unable to react, Marcia leapt forward to grab Ogg's leg just as he plummeted over the edge. Marcia's heroics only made things worse, as she too was now being dragged over the precipice. Polly dived, catching her friend's ankle just in time!

"I can't hold on!" screamed Marcia under the cumulative weight of Jake and Ogg.

A narrow shadow fell across her; the Izz-Ozz-Igg ladder deconstructing in midair to secure Ogg, who was still clinging onto the flailing Jake. In a few pulls, everyone was dragged back to safety.

"Thanks," breathed Jake, "that was a close one!"

"Too close," agreed Polly. "I think that's enough bungeeing for today."

"I was getting bored of it anyway!" grinned Jake.

Polly gave his shoulder a slap – playful enough to let him know that everything was all right, but hard enough to let him know that he'd better not do it again!

They continued upwards, all three now scrambling up the Izz-Ozz-Igg-Ogg totem pole. Amazingly, the brothers never complained or seemed to tire as they traversed ledge after ledge, with Jake once more leading the way. With only one ledge left before reaching the top, Jake let out a startled scream.

Polly, half-way up the Izz-Ozz-Igg-Ogg tower, scrambled to the top only to find Jake wrestling with a huge spider. The arachnid had pinned her brother to the floor, mandibles clicking menacingly inches from her brother's throat, Jake becoming trapped as he was swamped in fast spinning webs.

"Leave him alone!" ordered Polly, the bubble blower already in her hand.

The spider paused, probing her with unblinking eyes reminiscent of their stick man leader.

Was the spider smiling?

Polly thrust out her hand and held her ground.

The spider took a step towards her, its huge body completely overshadowing her brother. Inches from the ledge, Polly's resolve began to evaporate. There was nowhere for her to go. Still the spider advanced.

"Back!" yelled Polly.

Another step.

Not only was her resolve giving way, so were her legs as her knees began to knock. The spider grinned maliciously as it continued to press forward.

Out of options and out of time, there was no way she could do anything to defeat the spider. If she had some bubbles she might be in with a chance...

Four forms sprung from out of nowhere, somersaulting onto the spider's back and halting its progress. The startled arachnid bucked and squirmed, trying to dislodge its attackers, who had already looped some webbing around the spider's neck and were pulling with all their might. The giant spider struggled, a whirling vortex of legs, staggering to stay upright as the tourniquet tightened and tightened. Then, with a final convulsive shudder, the monstrous beast collapsed.

"Jake!" Polly rushed forward, her brother now completely covered by the giant spider's corpse. *"Help me!"*

The relieved smiles of the former stick men evaporated as they jumped off the spider to help.

"He's suffocating!"

Polly and the four brothers pushed with all their might, unable to shift the dead arachnid. They were running out of time. With no sound of movement coming from beneath the spider, Polly began to fear the worst. In sheer frustration, she stabbed into the black mass with her fist still holding the bubble blower. An oozing blackness dribbled down her right hand, the stench disgusting.

Polly didn't care; she began to weep, knowing that all was now lost. Surprisingly, the spider began to move – upwards!

The four brothers stared in disbelief as the huge spider slowly lifted clear of the ground, hovering inexplicably in the air.

Polly was already moving.

Jake lay motionless, still trapped in a sea of webs. Using the blower as a knife and tearing away with her hands, she ripped her brother free.

"Jake!" Polly shook her brother gently. "Jake, wake up, Jake! Please wake up!"

Jake remained unconscious.

"Jake, Jake, please wake up!" Polly collapsed onto her brother's chest.

"Is that a flying spider?"

Polly lifted her head.

Jake had opened his eyes and was looking on fascinated as the giant spider floated skywards. Polly jabbed her brother gently in the ribs before giving him a big hug.

"Easy, sis, I've already been crushed once today!"

"Sorry."

Jake sat up, rubbing his chest. "What happened? One minute I was being crushed by this big creepy-crawly, the next he's floating off in the sky."

"It's the Magic," said Izz. "There must have been some left."

Polly gazed down at the blower still in her hand, now stained black and sticky with spider blood.

"It whiffs a bit, doesn't it?" said Jake.

"No worse than you before a bath!" joked Polly, relieved that her brother was all right.

"Yeah," said Jake, "who'd have thought – flying spiders and Magic Bubbles!"

Marcia's voice floated up on the air. "Is anyone up there going to bother to help me?"

Chapter Eleven

CATAPULTS, BIRDS AND MUD!

The exhausted companions watched as Sor-Ben-Rez, floating above his enormous spider bubble punctured a hole through the mists.

A feeling of desolation and despair descended over everyone except Jake. He was already on the move, wasting no time in tying some webbing to a young sapling.

"Bring me some stones. It's time to bring old stick face back down to earth!"

After some frantic scurrying around, Jake was presented with a collection of stones from Izz, Ozz, Igg and Ogg, while Polly looked on with new admiration for her big brother.

Carefully selecting a stone, Jake placed it in the centre of the webbing before pulling back hard, aiming his impromptu catapult at the distant bubble. His first three attempts missed completely, but with a few careful adjustments, the next ones hit. The girls cheered then groaned as each one bounced harmlessly off the giant spider bubble.

Sor-Ben-Rez's distant cackling rained down, taunting their failed attempts.

"He's getting away!" cried Izz. "We need to try something else!"

"The box!" said Marcia, fishing out the small container with a triumphant flourish. "We must use the box!"

Everyone stared at Marcia, waiting to hear her plan. Marcia shifted her gaze from the ground to the disappearing spider bubble, and then to her companions, as the cogs inside her head clunked and whirred frantically searching for an answer. This continued for quite some time until finally her mental cogs found what they were looking for. "Fire it at the bubble. Quick before it's too late!"

Jake was a little hesitant, then suddenly everything clicked into place.

"Things above and things below sometimes come together!" said Polly and Jake in unison.

Jake placed the mud container into the catapult and began to pull back.

"Jake," Polly tapped her brother on the shoulder. "Don't miss!"

Jake managed a grin as he strained and took aim, pulling back even further. "Don't worry, Pol, I think I've got this—"

153

Jake slipped, launching the tiny container skywards. The small mud box arced high over the huge spider bubble, missing it completely. Instead, it caught Sor-Ben-Rez's smaller bubble, splattering mud all over its surface!

The thick mud began to ooze and spread, increasing in volume as it became

Thicker...

and Thicker...

and THICKER!

The spreading mud caused Sor-Ben-Rez's bubble to become **heavier** and **heavier**, and now sliding downwards around the circumference of the giant spider bubble, still tethered by its spider web.

Incandescent with rage, Sor-Ben-Rez dropped from his upside-down basket onto his half-mud-encased bubble, which was now hanging directly below the much larger spider bubble. All the while, the magical mud continued to creep up the sides of the bubble towards the seething stick man.

Sensing this was their chance, Polly instinctively pulled the bubble blower from her pocket. A tiny speck of soapy liquid glistened in the minuscule hole at the end. Polly's mind raced as she tried to figure out what to do. And then, in an instant, she knew!

"Jake, Marcia, I need you two to catapult me towards the spider bubble."

Marcia and Jake briefly exchanged *'Has she gone mad?'* looks, but Polly was already blowing, the tiny bubble growing Bigger...

and BIGGER...

and BIGGER...

Polly quickly climbed inside and after Izz, Ozz, Igg and Ogg had carefully manoeuvred the bubble into position on the catapult, they moved to help Jake and Marcia.

"No!" yelled Polly, "it's the Power of Three! Only Jake and Marcia must fire the catapult!"

The four brothers stepped aside reluctantly, worried looks etched on their faces.

Jake and Marcia strained at the catapult, drawing back the webbing further than ever before.

"Careful!" warned Polly, "You don't want to break it!"

Jake managed a grin, even though he and Marcia were pulling with all their strength. "You ready, sis?"

"As ready as I'll ever be."

"Okay, Marcia, on my count of three...

ONE...

TWO...

THREE!"

THWANG

Polly and her bubble were launched skywards; a bubble bullet heading straight towards the giant spider bubble. Unfortunately, Polly's bubble ricocheted right off the spider bubble, sending her soaring vertically upwards!

Polly's arms flailed wildly as her bubble zig-zagged uncontrollably. Everything was happening too quickly. Polly gathered herself, trying to get her bearings. At the same time, her bubble settled and moved less erratically. By now, the giant spider bubble was some distance below her. Polly shook her fist in frustration – as she did so, her bubble began to shake. Polly calmed herself down and with it, the bubble stopped shaking too. Something strange was happening. She looked down at her right hand – she was still holding the blower.

I wonder...

Polly stretched out her right hand to the right — instantly the bubble lurched to the right. Polly pointed out with her left hand to the left — Nothing. Polly stretched out her right hand across to the left — the bubble lurched left. She tried again, this time pointing straight up — the bubble soared upwards. Polly pointed downwards — the bubble dropped like a stone. The blower was guiding the direction of her bubble!

The giant spider bubble now some way below, she pointed towards it. Immediately, her bubble descended directly towards the spider bubble. In no time at all, Polly had successfully navigated herself directly on top of the enormous bubble crammed full with wriggling-jiggling spiders, their two bubbles now touching and joined together.

Polly now pointed the blower back towards Jake and Marcia. Slowly, the two conjoined bubbles began to change course, back towards the cavernous hole. From his position underneath the spider bubble, Sor-Ben-Rez screamed out curses and threats. Then suddenly, the cursing suddenly stopped. Jake and Marcia were shouting, but they were too far away for Polly to hear. She guessed from their frantic arm movements that whatever it was, it wasn't good.

Sor-Ben-Rez was up to something – *but what?*

"**H**e's using the pipe to blow another bubble!" yelled Marcia.

"It's no good, she can't hear you!" Jake, seeing that his sister had no idea what Sor-Ben-Rez was up to, scrambled around for more stones.

"What are you doing?" exclaimed Marcia. "We're running out of time. We've got to stop him!"

"That's exactly what I'm trying to do!" Jake had found a small flat thin stone. Placing the stony disk in the catapult, Jake took careful aim.

"Jake, you're aiming far too low – you're going to miss the bubb—"

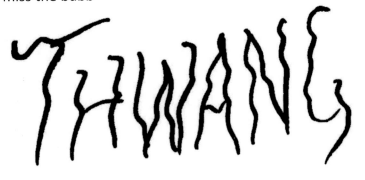

Jake launched the stone skywards. Marcia was right, it was much too low to hit the spider bubble. But that wasn't what Jake was aiming for. The stone cut through the air, smashing the pipe out of Sor-Ben-Rez's grasp – or more exactly, severing the stick man's hand still holding their Dad's pipe.

"AARRRGGHH!" Sor-Ben-Rez howled, first in pain and again, this time in anguish as the precious pipe fell away.

Far below, Jake and Marcia were cheering, but not for long. Sor-Ben-Rez was incanting something, his one remaining stick arm weaving and waving menacingly.

Polly had heard Sor-Ben-Rez's scream too. Mistakenly thinking that the threat was over, she continued to guide the giant bubble over the large cavernous hole far below, completely oblivious to Sor-Ben-Rez's spell casting.

Jake and Marcia looked on in horror as the stick man began to change shape, his form growing larger and darker with each passing second.

Polly, deep in concentration didn't see the dark shape looming above her as she guided the giant spider bubble into position.

A dark talon ripped through her bubble, clamping onto Polly's right arm before she could react. Outside, the giant black bird with a blaze of bright reddy-orange on its breast, flapped awkwardly, one of its massive wings obviously injured.

The bird's claws bit deeper into Polly's arm. Unable to take any more, Polly dropped the blower.

Immediately, the two bubbles began to gain height. The bird released its grip and began stabbing at her bubble sanctuary, its razor beak piercing the surface and yet somehow, her bubble remained intact. Seeing that his bubble-bursting attempts were going nowhere, the Sor-Ben-Rez bird plunged his head through the bubble, Polly somehow managing to dodge the lethal beak as the bird pressed further in through the bubble...

Closer and closer... until Polly found herself flattened against the bottom of the bubble to avoid being stabbed.

Sensing victory, the giant bird pressed again, its coal black eyes simmering with rage. Scrambling with frantic fingers, Polly tried desperately to reclaim the lost blower. Sor-Ben-Rez changed his angle of attack, first going for Polly's arm, then abandoning it altogether on spotting the blower. His beak just inches short, Sor-Ben-Rez couldn't quite reach the blower. The extra seconds of distraction were all that Polly needed. Sliding on her back along the bottom of the bubble, Polly grabbed the blower from underneath the bird's probing beak, then moving sideways, she thrust her hand up, plunging the blower as far as she could into bird's red-orange chest, hoping that the fragile blower wouldn't break in the process.

For the briefest of moments, the bird stopped motionless, its coal black eyes unflinching. Then slowly, its beak opened, contorting into the familiar twisted, sinister, snarling smile.

Sor-Ben-Rez and Polly's gaze locked together, both knowing that she was out of options.

The deadly bill now just inches away, opened wider and wider, ready for the killer blow. Foul smelling stale bird breath washed over her. Polly hoped the end would be quick, but somehow she doubted it.

Then, out of the blackness of the giant beak came something unexpected...

A bubble!

Small at first, then growing larger

and

larger...

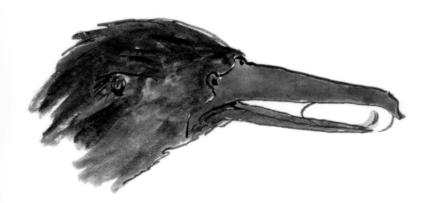

Try as he might, the Sor-Ben-Rez bird could not close its beak. Unable to breathe, let alone attack, the bird retreated, the bubble in its beak now beginning to weigh it down like a heavy translucent stone. Despite all its desperate flapping, even the bird's massive wings were unable keep it airborne. Unable to fly, the bird's hapless form slid around the surface of the giant spider bubble.

By now, the spider bubble was almost directly above the cavernous spider lair hole. With the blower still in her hand, Polly clenched her fist around it and pushed it against the lower side of her bubble. The soapy surface stretched, until finally her hand broke through. She wouldn't have much time. Opening her fist and gripping the gold top tightly, Polly stabbed down sharply into the enormous spider bubble.

The spider bubble exploded! Masses and masses of arachnids swamped and enveloped the giant bird as the dark spider cloud rained down into the cavernous hole far below.

It was then that Polly saw it. A smaller bubble with something inside rising up to meet her.

DAD'S PIPE!

Polly reached out, grabbing the pipe as it floated past, the small bubble pinging into non-existence. Using the blower to navigate her bubble, Polly steered down towards the catapult, where Jake and Marcia rushed to meet her.

Jake was beaming. "You did it, sis, you did it!"

Izz was peering into the cavern, a concerned look etched on his face. The others rushed to join him. As they looked over the precipice, spiders were already swarming up the sides.

"We have to seal up the lair and quickly. Mistress Pollyanna, you must use the Mechanism to blow a large bubble into the spider lair." Izz's three brothers nodded their anxious agreement.

Polly put the charred coloured pipe to her lips, which felt very odd indeed! She wondered what her Dad might think had he known what his daughter was doing with his dearest and most precious possession.

Images of her family cocooned in those dreadful cobwebs sent shivers down her spine.

"Mistress Polly, please, time is running out!"

Polly blew through the pipe.

Nothing happened.

Polly blew again.

Nothing.

The bubbles must have run out!

Polly turned to Izz in desperation. "They're all gone!"

Izz remained calm. "Try again."

"But—?"

"Mistress Pollyanna, please, you must try again."

Polly tried again.

Nothing.

Her mind raced – what could they do now?

Thoughts of her Mum, Dad and Joshy trapped forever as the world was overrun with nasty spiders flooded through her mind in a tsunami of horribleness. An torrent of rage filled her like never before!

"NO!"

Polly blew, her breath filled with a heady mixture of belief and desperation as it whistled through the ancient pipe.

Had her eyes not been closed, Polly would have noticed the char-black colour of the wood beginning to lighten.

"It's working!" cried Marcia.

Polly opened her eyes.

A small bubble was bobbling around just below the top edge of the pipe bowl.

Not wanting to take another breath for fear of losing the tiny bubble, Polly continued to blow. Wobbling around in the bowl like a fragile marble, the bubble began to expand, growing

BIGGER... and

BIGGER...
and
BIGGER...
and
BIGGER..

Dad's pipe was now back to its usual dark wood colour as the bubble toppled from the pipe and slowly descended into the cavern. After a few bounces and bobbles, the colossal transparent sphere settled firmly down, effectively sealing and plugging the spider lair.

"Good," said Izz. "Now we need some more mud." He turned to Marcia. "Miss Marcia?"

Marcia gulped. "I fired it at the spider bubble."

Izz smiled. "Yes, I know, but I think that you may still have it."

Marcia reached into her secret pocket, and to her surprise, pulled out the small mud box. Marcia gawped in disbelief. "How—?"

"We haven't much time, throw it onto the surface of the bubble."

Marcia hesitated, hypnotically staring at the container as if it were some prize jewel.

"MARCIA!" screamed Jake and Polly together.

The spell broken, Marcia flipped the top and tossed the small container into the cavern.

After a few bounces on top of the giant bubble, mud began to spill and then pour out, becoming

Thicker...

and

Thicker...

and

THICKER!

In a matter of seconds, the whole surface of the bubble and the remainder of the cavern was filled with tons and tons of thick oozy mud. As the mud increased, it began to solidify, until the giant hole ceased to exist, becoming a hard muddy impenetrable slab.

Chapter Twelve

THE POWER OF THREE

"**W**ell done, young lady, well done!" The King was striding towards her, arms outstretched. "I knew you could do it! I absolutely knew you could do it!"

Just behind the King was the Queen, resplendent in a flowing rose pink dress which matched the roses in her hair.

"Welcome back, Pollyanna. Welcome back, Marcia!" she said, greeting each of the girls with a smile. Both girls curtsied in turn. "And you must be Master Jake."

Taken completely by surprise and not quite sure what to do next, Jake dropped to one knee, his head bowed. "Your Majesty!"

The Queen stepped forward and held out her hand.

Jake took it and kissed it.

The Queen smiled graciously. "My dear, I was only going to help you back to your feet."

"Oh," said Jake, feeling more than a little silly.

Both girls giggled as Jake got back to his feet.

"You all have done a splendid job. Once again, we are all firmly in your debt." The Queen paused momentarily. "But things are not quite finished. We need the Power of Three. Pollyanna, do you still have the Magic?"

Polly held out the pipe and the bubble blower. "Your Majesty, we used the Power of Three just now."

The Queen looked confused.

"Me, Jake and Marcia," explained Polly, not sure that she was explaining anything at all well.

"Oh, I see," said the Queen, "that's not quite the Power of Three I was thinking of, my dear. Now, if you would be so good as to unscrew the top of the blower."

"It is unscrewed, the bottle is in Dad's pipe... er, I mean, the Mechanism," said Polly, before adding a little belatedly, "Your Majesty."

"Yes, Pollyanna, I know. You now need to unscrew the top from the blower."

Passing the pipe to Jake, Polly carefully took the needle-like blower and gave the gold top a gentle twist. To her surprise, the blower came free, revealing a small pin hole in the gold lid.

"Now, tap the top into the palm of your hand."

Polly tapped. A tiny golden seed tumbled out of the top.

"Wonderfully done, now it's time for the Power of Three," said the Queen.

The King's head bobbed excitedly in anticipation.

"But, your Majesty, I'm not sure what the Power of Three is."

The Queen smiled warmly. "I think you do, my dear."

"Yes! Yes! Yes!" agreed the King, breaking into an impromptu jig.

Polly was at a loss. She stared at the tiny seed glowing in her hand, not certain at all what to do. There was no Magic left—

Then she knew.

Reclaiming the pipe from her brother, Polly carefully dropped the seed into the pipe bowl. Then, lifting the pipe to her mouth, she blew, ever so gently, and as she did so, the vines covering the surface of the pipe began to change colour, from dark brown to vibrant green.

Polly continued to blow as the tiniest of bubbles began to emerge with the golden seed now hovering at its centre.

"The Power of Three! The Power of Three!" sang the King.

Up...

Up...

Up...

the bubble continued to rise, growing

Bigger...

and BIGGER...

and **BIGGER...**

the tiny seed becoming almost completely lost, if not for the fact that it was shining so brightly.

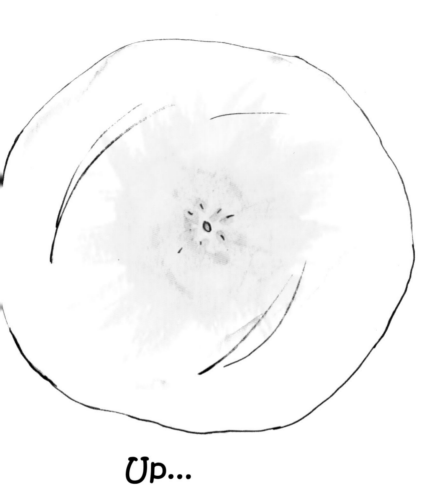

Up...

Up...

Up...

The bubble hovered high above the trees, directly over the freshly dried mud, with the golden seed growing

Brighter...

and BRIGHTER...

and BRIGHTER...

until not just the seed, but the whole bubble blazed like the sun and they could no longer look at it. Then, in a silent explosion that shook the trees and nearly blew them off their feet, the blazing light vanished.

Polly, Jake and Marcia gazed upwards into the clearest and bluest of skies, the mists now completely gone, as was the bubble with the golden seed.

"Wait!" said the King, his wiry body tense like a giant spring.

Everything was still, with nothing to be heard in the entire forest.

The King's eyes twinkled expectantly.

The small group of companions waited.

Then they waited some more.

Polly glanced over to the King with his twinkling eyes and beaming smile.

It was then that she heard it.

The tiniest of whispers...

Coming from the ground...

Coming from the freshly dried mud which suddenly fractured from its centre outwards, cracks

GROWING...

and
GROWING...

erupting all over its hardened muddy surface.

The tiniest of green shoots broke through the dirt, but it wasn't tiny for long.

Just like the bubble, it Grew...

and GREW...

and
GREW...

The whole ground rumbled as the mud exploded!
Shooting up into the sky was the most enormous Tree
that they had ever seen!

Higher...

Higher...

Higher...

the Tree sprang,
its branches laden
with golden fruit.

"The Power of Three," breathed Polly.

"Yes! Yes! Yes!" said the King, "The Seed, the Mechanism and the Magic! All had to come together for The Power of the Tree!"

The Queen sniggered most un-Queen like as she batted her husband's shoulder with a playful slap. "My dear, you are incorrigible sometimes!"

Then they all burst out laughing.

Polly ambled over to the newly formed Tree, gazing up through the branches as she ran her hand over the bark already knarled and knobbled and surprisingly old. The Tree felt warm and alive, almost as if it were breathing!

"It's alive," gasped Polly.

"Yes, dear," said the Queen, joining her. "A long overdue replacement." The Queen smiled a sad smile.

"The Tree of Darkness?" guessed Polly.

The warmth returned to the Queen's smile. "Your instincts are correct. It too was once as beautiful as this before the Darkness consumed it, strangling and choking until everything was gone."

"The Seed – it's from the Tree of Darkness."

The Queen nodded. "Before the Darkness and decay took hold, my good husband had the foresight to preserve its essence."

"And so he hid **the Seed** with the Bubbles!" finished Polly, her sudden epiphany leaving her feeling more than a little confused.

"He did indeed, and then promptly forgot about it," said the Queen, shooting her husband a fake look of disdain.

The King, looking suitably admonished tapped the side of his head with his finger. "Three hundred and twelve years of memories all stored safely in here!"

"With one or two becoming invariably lost," added the Queen, "for a while, at least! When the two of you were last here it didn't seem that important, but as the years went by, it was obvious that Sor-Ben-Rez hadn't been completely contained."

"Years?" interrupted Marcia. "But it was only a year since we were last here!"

"Seasons come and seasons go," replied the Queen, as if that explained everything.

It was Jake who spoke next. "You mean, time passes differently here?"

"Seasons come and seasons go," echoed the King, offering no more explanation.

Jake shook his head in wonder. "Amazing, it's almost as if—"

"Everything has been restored," finished the Queen, and indeed it was. The Queen smiled a radiant smile.

"Now, let's see if we can retrieve the Magic and put the Mechanism back together."

With a little help from Izz, Polly retrieved the bubble container from Dad's pipe, all the intricate vines covering it almost alive with vibrant green. Reassembling the blower and top, she screwed the bubble container back together. Meanwhile, the King took the pipe and reconnected the stem to the bowl, his fingers lovingly caressing the beautifully carved object.

"Now, it's time to make amends elsewhere," said the Queen. "First, my dear Marcia, we must do something about that poor dress of yours!"

Marcia looked down at her muddied top, torn and frayed at the edges. With a wave of the Queen's hand, the material not only began to mend, it also began to change, becoming a silky light replica of the same rose pink dress that the Queen herself was wearing.

"Wow!" breathed Marcia. "It's beautiful! Thank you, your Majesty!"

"You are most welcome," smiled the Queen warmly, "and most assuredly deserving of such a gown!" She turned her attention to Jake. "And what of you, Master Jake, what would be your reward?"

Jake was caught completely off guard by the Queen's question. *What could he possibly ask for?*

"A BOOK!" said the King, stepping forward to hand a stunned Jake a small leather-bound book, its soft green cover intricately embossed with leaves and branches.

"Thank you, your Majesty."

"It contains things you might want to know," said the King, "lots of important things."

Jake beamed, running his fingers over the delicate cover. "I'll take good care of it."

"And well you should, young man, for in it are untold treasures waiting to be discovered."

Jake trembled visibly with excitement.

The Queen turned to Polly. "And last, but certainly not least, what for you, Pollyanna?"

"Please, your Majesty, I just want my family back."

The Queen regarded her tenderly. "Don't worry, my dear, all will be restored, and more besides."

Polly breathed a sigh of relief. "There's still something that puzzles me," she said, Polly's curiosity bubbling to the surface. "The pipe... why Dad's pipe?"

The Queen smiled. "It didn't always belong to your father, Pollyanna. A long, long time ago, the pipe's home was here, right in the heart of Dizzelwood, as part of the Magic. Then one day, it mysteriously vanished."

"It must have been that nasty Sor-Ben-Rez," chipped in Marcia.

"Unlikely, my dear," said the Queen. "This was before his time, although I suspect that there may have been some 'ancestral' connection concerning the pipe's mysterious disappearance."

"So the pipe was lost then," said Polly.

"For a while, yes, but then my husband here managed to locate it."

"Yes, yes!" echoed the King excitedly, "Two things, two things!"

"Two pipes?" asked Marcia.

"No, not pipes," said the Queen.

"Me," said Polly.

"There's two of you???" exclaimed Marcia, her jaw dropping as she stared in disbelief.

"Me and the pipe, silly!"

"Oh," said Marcia, her cheeks blossoming deep red.

The King nodded. "You and the pipe, indeed!"

"So, that's why—"

"You got the bubbles," finished Jake.

"Yes, yes, the **ancient Magic** drew me to you!" beamed the King.

"But shouldn't it have been my Dad?"

"No, my dear, it was definitely you!"

"But my Dad had the pipe."

"Indeed, but you, my dear, had the heart! Not only that, but bucketfuls of courage too – and not just you." The King swept his gaze across the three companions, "but all three of you!"

"**The Power of Three!**" grinned Jake.

Polly gave her brother a shove.

"Don't forget us!" said the four brothers in unison.

"**The Power of Seven!**" corrected Jake.

"Of course, of course, how could I possibly forget our four Royal Advisors?" The Queen nodded a salute towards the beaming brothers. "Once again you have proved your loyalty and diligence above and beyond the call of duty, and in so doing, have become an even more valuable part our own dear family."

The brothers glowed with pride.

187

"And speaking of families, I'm afraid it's time for our friends to go home to rejoin their own families." The Queen extended a regal hand towards Polly. "Come, dear, take my hand."

Polly offered the Queen her right hand. The Queen's hands were soft and unbelievably warm, washing away the stinging throb in Polly's hand. Polly knew instinctively that the wound from the nasty spider bite was healed. The warmth continued to grow, spreading rapidly up Polly's arm and drenching her entire being with the most amazing warmth, like a great big, invisible snugly blanket!

Chapter Thirteen

THE RING AND THE BOOK

Polly opened her eyes. She felt warm and safe as she pulled her blanket over her head.

What a extraordinary dream!

There was a dim green light coming from her hand. A ring, green and delicate and a perfect fit on her ring finger. Polly twisted it idly. A fresh wave of warmth spread from her hand all through her body.

It wasn't a dream at all!

Then she noticed – she was fully dressed! Throwing back the bedclothes, Polly sat on the edge of her bed to examine her hand closely. No sign of any bite marks whatsoever. She gave the ring another twist, releasing more magical warmth. Polly had never felt so happy.

There was a knock on the door.

"Pol, are you in there?"

"Come in, Jake."

Jake wandered in, closing the door behind him. Her brother looked different somehow, maybe it was the lightness in his manner. His face beamed as he sat down next to her.

"Dad's found his pipe, but now he's complaining that it's full of soap. Every time he gives it a puff, tiny bubbles come out!" They both laughed. "He likes the new green colour, even though at first he thought it was all mouldy!"

Everything was back to normal!

Polly held out her hand. "Jake, look!"

"Wow, your hand's completely healed!"

"No, not that, the Ring!"

Jake's eyes widened. "It must be from the Forest Queen, speaking of which..." Jake reached into his pocket. "I've got the Book here."

The pocket-sized Book began to grow until it was big enough for both of them to hold it.

Polly's insides bubbled with excitement as she and Jake flicked through the pages, marvelling at the weird and wonderful things they read. They chuckled at the secret memories of their shared adventure together (something they would do many times over the coming months)!

Not only had Polly received a Ring and Jake a Book, but she and her brother were now closer than ever! She wondered how things were in Dizzelwood – was everything all right?

A sudden warmth radiated from the Ring causing Polly's heart to leap in her chest.

Everything was fine.

Not only that, everything was back to normal at home too, with no sign of any cobwebs or malicious spiders. Both Polly and Jake had gently probed their Mum and Dad for anything out of the ordinary, but no one had any memories of anything unusual, and if they did, they never spoke of it. As always, Marcia wanted desperately to say more about their adventures, but she was sworn to secrecy by Polly and Jake.

Everyone else may have forgotten, but Polly, Jake and Marcia's memories would live on forever!

Polly reached into her pocket. The familiar shape of the tiny container was wrapped in something.

Taking the container out, Polly unwrapped the old piece of yellowed paper:

The Magic and Book are yours to keep!
The Ring binds us together.

KEEP THEM VERY, VERY SAFE

Come back and see us again soon!

Look out for

Polly's next Great Adventure...

The Secret Leaves

Tomser Cat

home of brilliant
children's books

www.tomsercat.com